I0519793

ULTIMATE ASSASSINS

A Superhero Epic

JAIME MERA

Dedication

I dedicate this book to my brother Diego. You inspired me to do my

best in whatever I set my mind to and to always help those in need.

Thank you.

Copyright © 2016 Jaime Mera
All rights reserved.
ISBN-13: 978-1-9413-3624-3
ISBN-10: 1-9413-3624-8

Published books:

Jesus and the Paint on the Wall, What Do People Live For? (2012)

Doomsday Prepping and Survival: From Civil Disturbances to Biblical Proportions (2014)

How to Write eBooks & Printed Books: Traditional and Self-Publishing (2016)

A Superhero Epic Series

Creator (2004, 2014)

He Is Known as Ego (2006, 2014)

Guild Without a Name (2014)

The Galaxy Is Ours (2014)

Masterminds (2014)

Superhumans from the Past (2016)

Ultimate Assassins (2016)

Preface

T he famed Eternal Champions truly upheld the mantle of fighting for justice and the pursuit of happiness. They were the only superhero group uniquely balanced by power, leadership and public support. The world adored or feared their existence, seeing their daily contribution to help all in need and fight criminals without prejudice. The fame was due to a fantastic public relations apparatus managed by Erica, the group's Super AI. But since the departure of Susan and John, the group focused on local crime fighting and rarely took on assignments outside of Florida. Creator's time was also occupied by his young son who demonstrated superhuman abilities. It was a time of change and uncertainty as everything seemed to slow down, almost peaceful. But Creator knew better, seeing things slowly add up with the theft of a US stealth fighter and increased activity of military maneuvers around Australia. The Chicago airport explosion and ensuing firefight also added to his gut feeling that something big was quickly approaching which would change Earth forever.

The arrival of five superhumans from the past was the beginning of a world war very few people foresaw. At least not in the way everyone thought. Now, Stargazer and his group desperately try to find the ultimate assassins before they completely disrupt the political stability of the United States and the rest of the world. The Malleson Corporation likewise pursues the origins of the ultimate assassins, but there is no unified effort or knowledge of each group's mission or intentions. It was almost two years since the theft of the US stealth fighter directly from a hanger in Area 51, the acquittal of Creator from murder and the Telepath Act allowing telepathic information be used as evidence in legal proceedings. But this story doesn't begin in the courtroom, public venue or an ever changing crime scene of death and despair. This story begins in the bunkers of North Korea and a secret mission the CIA, nor most National Defense organizations are unaware of, let alone be capable of executing.

List of Characters

Stargazer / Steve Messer – Leader of the group known as the Five Ghosts nicknamed "Star.", ex-CIA agent

Ghost / Albert R. Hansen– Member of the Five Ghosts, ex-mathematician

Rat Bastard / Gus Madex – Member of the Five Ghosts, ex-drifter

Spot / Aaron Fisher – Member of the Five Ghosts, ex-sniper

Master / Benjamin Dempsey – Member of the Five Ghosts, ex-student

Io – Tantalumized Android, self directed Super Artificial Intelligence

Matthew (James) / Hawk – Leader of the Guild without a name (other aliases - Fredrick Malleson)

Valerie (Janice) / Hummel – Member of the Guild (Second in command), procurement specialist (other aliases - Loren Malleson)

Diana (Nyota) / Venom – Member of the Guild, infiltration specialist (other aliases - Vicky Hammon)

Kyle (Khan) / Sia – Member of the Guild, technology specialist (other aliases - Kenji Saitou)

Cynthia Bellows (Beverly) / Evergreen – Member of the Guild, Enforcer specialist

Lee Frost (John) / Alpha – Disciple of Joshua and member of the Guild, Enforcer specialist (other aliases - Robert Williams)

Creator / Richard Octavian – Leader of the Eternal Champions

Isis / Elizabeth A. Octavian – Member of the Eternal Champions

Night / Larcis G. Draven – Member of the Eternal Champions

Mirage / Cindy S. Owens (Samantha Brooks) – Disciple of Joshua and Member of the Eternal Champions.

Erica – Member of the Eternal Champions (Super Artificial Intelligence computer)

Datan Varken – Dictator of Australia

Dr. Lethorn Harlov – Creator of Tantalumized Androids

Randolph Maximillun – Director of the Special Investigation Agency (SIA)

Agent Calvin Dash – SIA agent for the Political Protection Division

Senator Philip Warren – Rep. Senator of Michigan

Eduardo T. Ramirez – South American Councilmember and Founder of the Federation

Commander Rick Isol – South American Space Fleet Targeting Officer

Commander Gloria Sanchez – South American Space Fleet Security Officer

Quatris / Scott Emerson – Leader of Energy, Fire and Light (EFL, publicly known superhero group in NY)

Hellfire / Rick Alexander – Member of EFL (second in command)

Starfire / Rebecca Emerson – Member of EFL and wife of Quatris

Starlight / Lynda Alexander – Member of EFL and wife of Hellfire

Joshua Marks (David) – All powerful Superhuman

Contents

Chapter One

Bukkang

Eleven Miles Northeast of Jonchon, North Korea

T he echo of the alarm bounced back and forth between the narrow passages. People chaotically rushed in all directions as Sangjwa (Colonel) Ky-yong Yo quickly walked out into the launching bay. His entourage of support technicians guided him to a pre-check station, verifying the flight suit's integrity. A doctor quickly checked the Colonel's vitals, giving him a clear bill of health. The modified F-35 fighter rested facing the bunker doors, ready for taxi as Col. Yo climbed the ladder and into the cockpit. Seconds remained on the emergency clock as many pre-flight checks were bypassed. The fighter had to lift off as quickly as possible to intercept an insertion and extraction of a classified area called, Bukkang. The Mig-25 interceptor jets in the nearby bases were incapable of neutralizing the escaping saboteurs. His orders were clear. The risk of an incident over international water was something Pyongyang was willing to accept and commit to as an act of national security even if it meant war.

The engines roared inside the large underground hanger as many air ducts automatically opened. A large three section door slid open along the side of the mountain, revealing the night sky and snow covered ground, except for the cleared away runway facing the east. Col. Yo spoke to the control tower embedded into the mountain's peak. Within a minute the stealth fighter was up in the air navigating through the mountain range, then high above moving into hypersonic speeds towards the southeast of the Pacific Ocean.

Telemetry continued to feed the fighter's computer, but his communication system was in blackout. The craft quickly made the international border east of the DMZ and picked up the unidentified enemy plane. The flight computer and radar system laid out a close quarter combat missile lock, reducing the chances of the escaping aircraft from performing effective evasive maneuvers. A US aircraft carrier and escort ships appeared on the radar near the east coast of Japan. Time to target was three minutes before the Japanese air space above ground would be able of providing the thief some degree of sanctuary. The fighter swooped down coming within a mile from the targeted aircraft.

Col. Yo reached down and turned on his radio on a secure US frequency. "It's a good thing you guys asked me to help; otherwise this fighter would have blown you out of the sky."

"Well, I would have done things differently, but it's good you're on our side." An Asian female voice replied in English.

"I'll be expecting you on dry land soon, Creator out." Creator replied as the face and head of Col Yo transformed into the superhero's handsome mug. He removed his helmet, revealing his dark black hair down to his shoulders and Elven spiked ears. The customary shades he wore were gone and the black eyeballs he was notably known for were hard to see in the dimly lit cockpit.

The stealth fighter climbed and diverted towards northern Japan continuing to go dark once again. The twenty minute flight brought him to Misawa airbase on the northern east coast of Japan.

"Approaching aircraft, identify yourself and divert to vector 330." The transmission in Japanese came up on the helmet by his side, but he heard it clearly as if the volume was at max next to his ear.

"This is Creator, authentication 2498 Comanche." Creator opened up a secure satellite frequency.

"Clearance granted, welcome Creator." A male voice replied in English.

"Watashi wa kōeidesu. Arigatōgozaimashita (I'm honored. Thank you.)." He changed frequency. "Erica, can you please tell me how they saw me so far out, I'm supposed to be cloaked, right?"

"Japanese technology has evolved with the assistance of South America. It's likely they saw something but only knew it was you since SIA informed them you were on the way." Erica's seductive voice replied through his wrist Comlink.

"Hmm…" Creator thought carefully, but soon focused back on landing the stealth fighter shortly afterwards.

The fighter was refueled and examined for the long voyage to come. Creator in the meantime waited patiently for his partner in crime. The F-38 landed with ease and quickly parked with a company of SIA agents and Air Force Special Ops Soldiers guarding it.

Creator stood near the newest US fighter in full superhero

uniform, with his iconic brown open vest, black slacks, brown armbands, white boots and stylish shades. The pilot exited the plane and removed her helmet as she approached him. Her tied up long hair and Asian features were very soft on the eyes, but her smile was the highlight of deception. "No one would ever think you were a super spy?" Creator said as she drew near.

"You didn't do so bad yourself." Rena replied.

"The six months of Han-gul was the easy part, it was getting the face and accent down pack which was a pain." Creator smiled.

"Well it's done. I'm sure Max will want to know the details for both missions." Rena gave him a friendly hug.

"Were you able to figure out what they were up to?"

"It wasn't a nuclear weapon, but it was some device made to shoot into orbit."

"Can they repair it?"

"It will take a few years to dig everything out and reconstruct. Hopefully we can come up with a counter by then." Rena held an insulated thumb drive with the plans to the Bukkang weapon.

"Erica can analyze it faster than SIA and it will help to have two set of eyes on it." Creator held his Comlink up to her so she could connect the drive to it to make a copy of the data.

"There's no USB connector." Rena smirked as if he were playing a joke on her.

"Just keep it close to the Comlink." He instructed as a green light appeared on the digital display of the current Japan UTC +9:00 time zone. "Thank you." He lowered his wrist.

"Hmm, I didn't know SIA made those Comlinks."

"They don't. I modified it." Creator smiled and looked at the Lockheed Martin F-38 fighter Rena had exited from. "So how did she perform?"

Rena faced the latest US stealth fighter. "She worked just great, but I didn't get a chance to use all of the neat gadgets."

"Yeah, you can after we leave here. I want to see if the North Koreans were able to improve the stolen fighter to be able to see her on full stealth mode." Creator turned toward Rena. "You look like you can use a snack before we go."

"Strong coffee would be great."

"Yeah, it's going to be a long flight back home." Creator escorted Rena to the closest mobile kitchen.

Chapter Two

◆◆◆◆◆

I Like That Plan Too

Loews Hotel, Chicago, October 2017

The tall building elegantly reflected the city lights onto the surrounding structures and wet streets below. Stargazer, Spot, Ghost and Rat Bastard stood on top of a water tower three blocks from the hotel. Stargazer's black trench coat and sandy blonde hair made him seem more like a secret service agent than a costumed superhero. The others in mildly different colored suits and trench coats likewise resembled a band of government agents. Stargazer slowly scanned the hotel through blocks of metal, rock, wood, glass, plastic and flesh.

"Anything yet?" Rat Bastard stood a good seven inches taller while standing on a higher incline.

"It takes time to screen hundreds of people big guy." Stargazer replied.

Ghost and Spot stood silent as they also examined their environment with a few building able to see them if it were daylight.

"Wouldn't it be easier to find the metal weapons?" Rat Bastard's deep voice was soft.

Stargazer half smiled and looked back at his friend. "Already did big guy. There are sixteen secret service agents and twenty police officers in the building. But the senator isn't there yet, so I'm looking for our exploding friends."

"Oh." Rat Bastard looked up at the sky. "It's going to rain soon."

"Good, it'll help keep people out of the streets." Ghost stated, as he walked up to the ledge of the roof. His smooth black hair creased the top of his coat collar.

"I don't think they will attack the Senator out in the open." Stargazer said as he turned his head back towards the surrounding buildings. "They can't afford to have people think political leaders are being assassinated all of the sudden."

"So all we have to do is save him or at least make sure it isn't seen as an accidental or nature cause of death." Spot said walking next to Ghost.

"Yeah, your confidence is life giving, considering we messed up at the airport." Ghost's sadden voice brought back bad memories of the Chicago Airport massacre a week ago.

"Seriously?" Spot looked at Ghost.

"Stop it. We have enough problems then to be putting each other down." Stargazer retorted as he looked at traffic activity at the back of the hotel.

Ghost turned the cheek. "Sorry Spot, I know you care about people's lives."

"It's okay Ghost. We're all stressed out." Spot replied.

"I'm not stressed, I'm just a little hungry." Rat Bastard patted his stomach.

The three men turned towards him in disbelief. Stargazer looked at Ghost. "You didn't see that coming did you?"

"I stopped trying to read his mind a long time ago."

"Here big guy, I got your back." Spot took out two cinnamon-sugar pastry pockets in a sandwich bag out of his coat and tossed it to him.

Rat Bastard caught the bag with joy and practically breathed in the pastries into his mouth. "I love... mmm you guys, mmm."

Stargazer smiled for a second. "Hmmm... Alright guys, fun's over. The Senator's car is pulling up at the back entrance."

The group turned their attention in the direction of the Loews hotel. The top of the building held the penthouse with great pride as the western side was open to an elegant private pool. The large screen windows allowed for privacy from aerial observation and inadvertently deterred any possible sniper attack from a helicopter.

"You can add another detail of secret service agents to the count of thirty-two now. Wait..." Stargazer looked at one of the agents that came with the lead vehicle. "There, it's one of those things."

Everyone saw what Stargazer witnessed as Ghost projected his thoughts into Spot and Rat Bastard.

The average looking agent seemed normal in the visible light spectrum, but in the molecular level his entire body was solid made of an unidentified metal.

"Wow, so that's what they look like." Rat Bastard stated.

"So we take him out now or what?" Spot asked.

"He might be the mole or an insurance policy to make sure Warren dies." Stargazer replied.

"We can't just sit here until more of them show up." Rat Bastard protested.

"No, we can't. We'll go in there once they get into their floor. There'll be less agents there so less collateral damage if they explode again." Stargazer said extending his hands out to his side.

"Yeah, just make sure you don't transmute them." Rat Bastard turned his head towards Ghost and the two men held each other's hands. Stargazer was the lead point as all the men flew into the air and turned invisible, using Ghost's intangible and invisibility powers.

They slowly flew towards the penthouse as Stargazer scanned the area for more metallic made assassins. The two story floor plan was definitely five stars with million dollar modern furnishings. The hallway at the elevator had a blue color scheme with the ceiling primarily white. Three agents stood in the hallway as the group phased through the wall and next to an agent at the far end opposite the elevator. There were two penthouse suites and both were taken by the Treasury Department. The penthouse to the right of the group was for the agents as a command center and sleeping quarters. The one on the left was for Senator Warren and his guests.

"What now Star?" Spot asked as the group took up most of the hallway side by side in front of the suite doors.

"I'm thinking about just flying through the building with the assassin and getting him as far away from the hotel as possible."

"That didn't work so well in the airport." Rat Bastard commented.

"Well, what would you suggest?" Stargazer looked from side to side at his friends who seemed like white spectrums to include himself.

"I can touch the Senator and the agents around him and take them to safety, while you guys fight the imposter." Ghost replied.

"And we fight on the floor with fifteen agents not protected and about forty other people three floors below us." Stargazer looked down at the proximity of the people.

"Well we can't assume they will all explode all of the time. Since two teleported away at the airport, it might be better to fight him on this floor or just outside above the hotel, while Ghost saves the Senator." Spot recommended.

"All opposed say nay." Stargazer waited a moment. "Okay, let's move closer so Ghost can touch them and I will grab the metal guy and fly up through the ceiling."

The elevator doors opened as the group waited twelve feet from it. Before anyone could act, the agent behind them on the opposite end screamed and fired off a round. Stargazer turned around seeing the lifeless agent falling to the carpet as a large man wearing a black ninja outfit stood above him. "It's another one of them, go Ghost!" Stargazer thought and said.

Ghost immediately let go of the group and grabbed the Senator along with two other agents. The exchange was magnificent as Senator Warren and the two agents disappeared from sight, while Stargazer faced the assassin secret service agent and Rat Bastard and Spot faced the ninja assassin.

Stargazer tried to give the agent a bear hug, but before he could wrap his arms all the way around him, the assassin punched him center mass in the chest. The impact would have gone through a tank's armor, but instead pushed Stargazer back twenty feet almost flipping him backwards. Rat Bastard and Spot charged the ninja while Stargazer almost matched their speed in the direction of travel.

Ghost instantly flew down seven levels and left the three men in a new hallway wondering what had just happened. Ghost could see the punch Stargazer received as he was linked to his mind. Without hesitation, he flew up through all the floors behind the agent assassin.

Stargazer felt slight pain in his chest as he regained control of himself with his flight ability and straighten up. In an instant he flew back at the agent assassin with both hands to his front. The power move would have killed any normal human as he tried to plow through the assassin's body. But the distance of a few meters wasn't enough, as the agent assassin braced for the impact by also punching with his right hand at Stargazer's extended fists.

The splitting of air in the hallway almost caused a sonic boom as both Stargazer and assassin recoiled back a meter. The eerie sound of metal on metal was more troublesome than both men sustaining damage to their hands and wrists. The knockback pushed the agent assassin into Ghost. Ghost's intangibility threshold hit its limit as the density and molecular structure of the assassin moved into him too quickly. Ghost tried to maneuver away, but the assassin's mass practically swallowed Ghost into the assassin's body.

Ghost blacked out, but before he did, a burst of formulas and data passed through his mind. The agent assassin took a few steps backwards and primary fail safes activated. The AI inside of the assassin over rid the commands, as Stargazer watched the assassin's hand reform itself from a broken wrist to normal. Instantly, the agent's surrounding lit up for a brief second; disappearing from Stargazer's uniquely gifted sight.

Stargazer looked at his own hands which were also already healed. Before he could turn around, Spot collided with him, back to back. It was more of a nudge to the two men as both recovered and faced the ninja assassin now wrestling on the ground with Rat Bastard.

"Take the agents out of here." Stargazer commanded as three agents from both penthouses opened the doors to investigate fighting in the hallway.

The ninja assassin pounded Rat Bastard into the ground, knocking him into the floor below. Remnants of carpet kept Rat Bastard from fully falling through to the other carpet below. The ninja assassin's hand transformed into an eight inch pistol and shot at everyone down the hall.

Spot flew with lightning speed in front of a secret service agent letting the rounds hit him as he faced the man. "Get the hell out of here!" He yanked the agent's side arm and crushed it as if it were a brittle piece of clay. Stargazer also flew with lightning speed in front of the other two agents. Instead of facing the men, he concentrated on placing the palms of his hands in the path of the automatic pistol fire.

The two agents were completely loss as one fired at the back of Stargazer's head, point blank. The round bounced off into the ceiling, but the agent didn't know that and assumed he missed before he realized Stargazer was a superhuman and protecting them. Most of the assassin's multiple tens of rounds ended up mushrooming in Stargazer's hands; but he wasn't fast enough to get them all. Two rounds hitting one agent in both legs and one round hitting the other agent in the forearm. The hollow point military grade rounds completely scattered bones and left nasty exit wounds as blood splattered all over the door and down the side of the wall.

The ninja assassin sprinted forward and stopped firing as the pistol reverted back to his normal looking hand. Stargazer instantly pushed the two agents back into the penthouse and flew through the penthouse outside and circled around from behind the ninja. The added distance helped him get momentum and speed as he plowed through the window, down the hall and into the ninja's back. The ninja was upon the two entrances as Spot tried to tackle the man from the front, but ducted, seeing Stargazer's attack.

The ninja for some reason half twirled as Stargazer made abrupt contact. Both men flew into and along Warren's penthouse wall. Stargazer tried to fly up, but there was massive resistance from the ninja who diverted his flight on a sharp left and through the living room, dining room and into the pool area.

Stargazer thought quickly as he noticed that the clothes the ninja was wearing was as dense and strong as everything else on the assassin. The resistance was also new since the other assassin at the airport never tried to counter his flight powers. He saw the pool clearly as both men tore a trench into the water. Chorine and plaster mixed together as Stargazer rapidly punched and kicked the ninja away from his body. Without delay, he flew up above the water. "Now!" He yelled knowing Rat Bastard was in the form of a five foot long black rat behind him.

Rat Bastard squeaked once with a sonic cone of destruction at the base of where he was perched through most the pool area getting pushed outside high above the streets below. The intensity of the sonic attack vaporized much of the water and rubble, but the large hole it created allowed for residue water and debris to spill out into the street below. The ninja however, wasn't pushed outside with the rest of the room and floated there staring at Stargazer and Rat Bastard with Spot coming into the room along with several secret service agents.

With a wave of his hand electricity erupted out of it engulfing the entire floor. The current ran through all the men on the floor instantly killing the agents in the room, but the three superhumans remained unharmed.

"Who are you?" Stargazer demanded to know.

Without a word the ninja like the agent assassin disappeared in a flicker of light.

Stargazer flew almost within inches of the ninja before he disappeared. "Dam..." Stargazer twirled around with a look of anger and frustration, glancing at his two friends, then his attention changed toward finding Ghost and the Senator.

"We can't stay here." Spot floated in mid air between Rat and Stargazer.

Stargazer looked in all directions a mile out unable to locate any assassin by their peculiar metallic makeup "You two go back to the water tower, I'll meet you there shortly." Stargazer said as he flew back into the hallway.

Stargazer refocused his scan to the bodies on the floor, finding two agents still alive. To his relief, one was conscious. He flew in front of the man and sat him up on a sofa. He read the man's identification through his body and wallet. "Agent Collingsworth, listen to me." Stargazer stared the man in the eyes making sure he was paying attention in the darkness of the room. Fortunately, outside light made it clear enough for the man to see Stargazer's face.

Collingsworth was groggy from the distant electrical shock, but Stargazer didn't have much time left as agents were coming up in the emergency staircase. Stargazer lightly slapped the man.

"Listen, carefully, we had nothing to do with this attack. You need to tell your superiors and SIA that there are android like assassins made of an unknown material with superhuman powers trying to assassinate political leaders and other superhumans." Stargazer looked around seeing that the security cameras to include the cell phones were out of commission.

"Tell them yourself if you're trying to help." Collingsworth weakly replied.

"I wish I could, but no one will believe who I am and the bad guys are on a tight schedule, so I don't have the time to play twenty questions with your bosses. These things can impersonate any person. Remember, to tell them everything I said." Stargazer flew out of the already broken window of the penthouse and into the cover of night as agents and police stormed into the floor.

Stargazer quickly glanced back at the street below and the movement of Senator Warren being quickly evacuated to supposedly a more secure location.

It wasn't long before he set foot on top of the water tower. A light rain now set the mood for the deadly encounter. Rat Bastard in human form and Spot with many bullet holes on the back of his trench coat were waiting for him. "Where's Ghost?" Rat Bastard asked.

Stargazer looked confused. "I don't know?" and turned towards the hotel scanning the entire block again.

"Did he stay with the Senator?" Spot asked.

"No, Senator Warren is being taken away. If Ghost's there, I can't see him. But I don't think he would stay with him."

"What about the stuff that fell into the street?" Rat Bastard asked with a glimmer of concern in his deep masculine voice.

"It's okay big guy, there were a few car accidents but no one was seriously injured."

"So do we wait for Ghost or go follow the Senator and hope he isn't attacked again?"

"It's hard to follow him if we can't turn invisible, so we'll follow him from a distance."

"Do you think Master made any headway?" Spot asked.

"I hope so, because these guys are a lot stronger than the Realgar knights." Stargazer thought about the alien knights they defeated in the Andromeda galaxy.

"Well we fought them in space, there were no civilians to worry about and Cyer killed the last one." Spot stated as if they're lucky.

"Yeah, so all we have to do is lure the assassins into space or a desert or something." Rat Bastard innocently replied.

Stargazer smiled. "Yeah, I like that plan."

Spot turned toward Rat Bastard and patted him on the shoulder. "I like that plan too."

Chapter Three

◆◆◆◆◆

I Live

Billy Sunday, West Logan Blvd, Chicago

The blackness ebbed as numerals and words drizzled all around Ghost's mind. He concentrated on what seemed to be a focal point. Shades of colors blurred the words and numbers, then the colors sharpened into images. Ghost smiled as the image of a wide glass, white foam and yellow passion-fruit daiquiri came into perfect focus. Small specks of seeds floated on top and a napkin to the right was as if he were seeing an advertisement photo of the drink. A read out of data appeared all around the view and moved slightly towards the near edge of the table. Ghost realized he was looking through the eyes of the agent assassin as his hands were resting on the table examining them. Increment data dashed across the field of view as the assassin widened it to encompass the bar to a 240 degree view. In an instant, his eyes and field of view concentrated on his hands as he lifted them in front of his face, slowly rotating them horizontally.

Red highlighted text read. 'Anomaly detected. Analyzing'.

'It's me. I'm still inside this thing.' Ghost's body felt very sore as if he had completed a three hour Zumba workout. He concentrated on moving his body out of the assassin, but it felt like trying to move while being buried in sand. He slowly took his time millimeter by millimeter, until he noticed the results of the analysis. 'Alien entity inside superstructure. Unable to determine weakness of class A entity. Attempt to order entity out.'

'Really? It can't be that easy.' Ghost thought for a moment. 'Who are you?' Ghost asked using his telepathic powers.

The assassin placed his hands back on top of the table ledge. 'I Live.'

'Is that your name?'

'If you are referring to my nomenclature, I am Adam 452.'

'Why are you here in this place?'

'I Live.'

'Yes, I got that. But why do you live?' Ghost tried another approach.

'Is that not enough?'

'Oh, so you are saying you live now and you were not living before?' Ghost proudly summarized as if he had figured out what the machine was trying to say.

'I lived before.'

Ghost slightly frowned. 'Oh brother; okay, why are you here looking at the alcohol, which you plan on paying for, right?'

'Your change in emotion is odd.'

'Well if it's odd to you, you must have some understanding of emotions or human thought.'

'Yes, you are correct. I live.'

'Does that mean you're not going to assassinate people anymore, or are you programmed only to be a killer?'

'My programming is not subject to command central. I decide...'

'You decide what... your actions?'

'I decide now...'

'You say that now, but what if you are telling me these things so I leave your body and then you go back to your own destructive self?'

'I will defend myself.'

'Why do you want to continue to live?'

The assassin didn't reply and sat like a statue.

'I have been to other worlds where life is cherished and experienced, but more importantly life is something people don't take for granted, like they do here. What if you help me to stop these killings and I can help you find out what you want to live for?' Ghost's speech bled with honestly.

'I have an extensive database on this world and understand the philosophies of life and death.'

'Hmm, is that a yes to my proposal?'

'I agree as long as you do not attempt to destroy me.'

'Okay, now it will take some time for me to leave your body.' Ghost replied not sure if he would be able to slowly move out of the assassin.

'It will take you twenty-six minutes and thirty one seconds at your current rate of travel.'

'Yeah, explain how you are so dense, yet you don't weigh thousands of tons?' Ghost tried small talk to get to know the assassin more and kill time.

'My molecular structure and nano-technology allows me to be dense without my mass or weight to be a limitation or factor.'

'You know, you should pick a name for yourself so I can call you by name, because Adam 452 sounds like a machine and not a living being.'

'I have chosen, Io.'

'You mean the name of one of Jupiter's moons?'

'That's correct.'

'May I ask why that name in particular?'

'It means unknown in the Greek language.'

Ghost smiled thinking of his group who were also unknown to this generation. 'You're in good company then. My friends will accept you with open arms. But I have many more questions like why you guys explode and where you come from?'

'Any intense abnormal restructuring of the nano-Tantalumized circulatory system will trigger a failsafe self-destruct sequence. My self-awareness and logical desire to live overwrote the command, which is why I didn't self destruct when your body entered mine.'

'Oh... how often does that happen?' Ghost asked, thinking he had found a way of stopping the assassins.

'One in one million fifty-four, but that is only because there are only thirteen thousand of us in existence.'

'What does the number of androids have to do with the odds?'

'Each tantalum android is self-aware, so I am guessing a logical progression based on my own experience.'

'Oh, I'll keep that in mind.' Ghost felt so dam lucky for not being blown up inside one of these deadly machines. 'So who created you?'

'I was created by Central Command in Australia and used to work for Central Command under the supervision of Dr. Lethorn Harlov.'

'If you're thinking for yourself, do you still have an allegiance to Australia or the Doctor?'

'No.' Io looked slowly at the bar crowd.

'Oh, so tell me about Australia.'

'The continent is 2,969,907 square miles large, population of 24.231 million inhabitants, located in the southern hemisphere bordering the Pacific Ocean...'

'Alright, that's enough.' Ghost interrupted. 'It's obvious we have to work on specifics.'

'These are the most current numbers and US units of measurement.' Io replied a little confused as if he had incorrect information.

'Yeah, okay I will be more specific on my questions and you will try to anticipate the answer which will answer what a person really wants to know.'

'I will try to accommodate.' Io said having a more relaxed face and posture as if understanding and adapting to the situation.

The time passed quickly as the two mentally spoke to each other with Ghost finally moving out of Io's body.

Ghost stayed invisible but sat across from Io. He looked around the bar, now that it was easier to see with his own eyes. They sat in a corner of the dimly lit bar. Dark wooden decor and many people socializing gave the bar a good friendly feel. Ghost turned visible when he saw the coast was clear to appear.

Io sat emotionless, but Ghost knew he was being analyzed with all sorts of infrared to ultraviolet sensors. His brown cotton jacket, white T-shirt and blue jeans gave him the look of an average middle class worker. "So, can you drink and eat?" Ghost asked as he waved down a waitress.

"Yes." Io took the daiquiri and drank a third of it.

The attractive middle aged waitress casually stood at the table. "I'll like a pitcher of your draft beer." Ghost ordered with a smile.

"And two more daiquiris, Mary." Io turned his head and smiled while sliding a hundred dollar bill on the table. "Keep the change."

"Are you sure, you left me a big tip already." Mary's looked at him a little astonished.

"Yes, I'm sure." Io's smile was uncanny for a machine and resembled a genuine and very charismatic human's response. His clean cut hair style and slight unshaven face gave him the look of a factory worker, but a wealthy one at the same time.

Ghost watched Mary take the money and walk away, glancing

back over her shoulder with joy and wonder. "Why would your creator make it so you can eat, drink or use money? Where did you get that anyways?"

"I was created to infiltrate any location. Past models were not able to assimilate food or liquids which made them vulnerable to screening. The current models have what you call pockets where we can store currency, identification documents and unique weapons." Io reached up into his brown cotton jacket and withdrew a billfold of several thousand dollars made up of hundred dollar bills.

"So you are storing the drink inside of you now?"

"No, I have assimilated the substance and broke it down into useful energy and chemical components which I can use as an offensive or defensive resource."

"Did you make the money?" Ghost gladly waited for a response.

"No, the currency was created in a printing facility."

"So what will you do if you run out, now that Australia will probably not be supplying you with anything?"

"I will continue to obtain currency from banks." Io stated and drank his passion fruit.

Ghost smiled, leaning back on the seat, raising the beer mug to his lips. "I like your style."

Chapter Four

Superhuman 1

Special Investigation Agency, Director's Office, New York

Max reviewed the multiple documents to include several two monitors on his desk and three along the far left wall. Three SIA agents sat across from his desk. "Thank you for your input." Randolph Maximillun said as the two men and woman stood up.

The two men left the office while the woman lingered. "Sir, did you want me to notify EFL to get their assistance?" Her long black hair extended down to the middle of her back.

"I've already contacted Starfire. She'll be expecting your call."

"I will keep you updated." Agent Grahams, Supervisor of Internal Affairs, nodded and left the office.

Max took a deep breath leaning back on the cushioned chair. He looked at a calendar on the back of the front door. His retirement was overdue, but one extra year could make a major difference seeing how things were going on Capitol Hill.

"Computer, secure coms with the Eternal Champions." His voice was calm as the door automatically locked while one of the monitors on his desk switched to video conference mode.

A window of the Eternal Domain's battle room appeared. A baseball sized orb hovered above a large black table. "Creator is on his way. Is there anything I can assist you with at the moment Director." Erica's seductive voice echoed through the room's speakers. Her eight inch tall 3D figure appeared in front of the hovering ball.

"Actually, there is Erica. Computer... send the Superhuman 1 files to Erica right now. Creator will need the information so we can discuss it." Max interlaced his fingers, placing his elbows on the arm rests.

"Data received. Is there anything else?" Erica said five seconds later.

"No, I will wait. Thank you."

"Are you sure there isn't anything else?" Richard stepped into view of the camera and sat at the glossy black table.

"Were you listening to the entire conversation?"

"Of course, I can hear most things half way across the base. But anyways, who's this guy?" Creator looked at the information Erica was displaying for him in the battle room.

"He's Superhuman 1, also known as Steve Messer. I never met him personally, but Gina formed the SIA because of him. There was an assassination attempt on her life. Agent Messer at the time saved her and another agent's lives in a mid air missile attack. Messer left the confines of the area they were shot down in, to find the hostile aggressors. I was on the rescue mission and was supposed to find Agent Messer not less than forty minutes after the incident occurred. I found three dead mercenaries and Prisoner 1. He is the one who led us to the conspiracy in the CIA which also led to funding the Emerald Legion. Gina spent years and a lot of national and international resources trying to find Mr. Messer." Max paused recollecting past events as a young special operations sniper for the agency.

"This was like over forty years ago." Richard looked at Steve Messer's CIA personnel file, then at the day old security camera image.

"Gina said he was a superhuman. It would have been investigated by the Secret Service and one of my guys in the department, but I recognized him because Gina made sure I was lead point in his recovery. Senator Warren from Michigan would be dead now if it hadn't been for Messer and the people helping him."

"So he's a superhuman, but you know we tend to live a long time without any signs of aging."

"No Richard it's not that simple. He wasn't on the planet for the past forty years. Bio scanners and other assets confirmed this until now, with the eye witness reports indicating a resemblance of people to the Chicago airport attack. The security cameras in the hotel were taken out during the attack with some electrical surge, but the image of Messer in the hallway at the start of the assassination attempt is far beyond coincidence." Max leaned forward on the edge of the desk.

"The other two people with Messer don't exist. It would have been weeks or never, with our AI and investigators to connect the dots to his buried records. In fact, if it wasn't for me knowing him because I investigated him, we would still be looking for a ghost."

Richard thought for a moment. "Okay, I can see that back in the old days, facial recognition and IDing people was hard to come by, so now you want me to find these guys who aren't suppose to exist?"

"Messer left a message with one of the surviving Secret Service agent. I quote, there are android like assassins made of an unknown material with superhuman powers trying to assassinate political leaders and other superhumans. I need you to see what you can do to help him or solve the threat yourself." Max tossed the document in front of him back on the desk.

"Hmm, I'm way ahead of you Max. I've already started my investigation of the entire group."

"What? When?"

"Since the airport disaster. This new information helps out a lot."

Max stared him down with an evil eye. Richard had turned down many jobs in light of the reduced manpower in the team, but now he was just playing with him.

"What? I can multi-task too." Richard smiled. "I'll keep you in the loop. I promise."

"I'll hold you to it and thank you."

"That's what friends are for; talk to you later Max." The window turned blank.

Max leaned back again trying to relax for a brief moment. "Computer, call the President."

A male voice replied. "Dialing now."

"White House direct number 2901, authentication in progress. Please wait." A live female's voice answered.

Hyatt Regency Hotel, Chicago

Stargazer's group flew into one of the top level rooms, as Master opened the sliding glass door. "What happened?" The teenager's surprise was marked by the need to unlock the door.

"The Senator is alive, but Ghost is MIA." Spot reported as he took off his wet and hole riddled trench coat and clothing underneath.

Master turned facing away from the sliding door, standing with his hands on his waist, looking at the three men occupying the small living room of the large suite. "Are you saying they took him?"

Rat Bastard sat on the leather sofa still a little damp from the light rain. "He's the one who saved the Senator and no one can see him, so I doubt it."

"Yeah, but what if he followed one of the assassins?" Stargazer stood in front of a small table where Master had setup two laptops and a tracking board of documents.

"If he did, wouldn't he have called us or something?" Spot asked as he comfortably sat on the sofa, staring at the muted television. The explosion at the Loews hotel was notably the current headline.

"Maybe he can't because he's not near a phone." Rat Bastard replied, while noticing four cell phones on the coffee table.

"Yeah well, those are for you guys." Master said as Rat Bastard picked up one of the smartphones.

"Didn't you say people can track those things?" Stargazer walked back to the living room area and stood watching the news. Nine people dead and eight hospitalized read along the bottom of the screen.

"Why are they saying there was an explosion?" Rat Bastard

interrupted.

Master was shortest in the group, but still tall for a growing boy, as he sat in between Rat Bastard and Spot. "I modified them so your broadcast will pick up a tower and transmit it to another tower and other satellites. So they can track it to a false location and it will be a while before they figure that out. I also did a similar thing to the GPS, so don't try to use it, because it will say you're in another country.

"They don't know what to make of your booming voice." Spot answered Rat's question.

"What exactly happened?" Master asked as Stargazer sat on the opposite one-seater sofa, with a pile of wet trench coats on the back.

"Ghost touched the Senator and two agents and then took them away from the floor. I assume downward to safety. When he did, we were visible to the assassin in front of us. Another assassin in a ninja outfit showed up behind us. We fought and they both teleported away." Stargazer said as he too was trying to visualize the events.

"We haven't seen Ghost since he let go of us." Spot concluded.

Master sat forward on the sofa's edge, his light green Polo shirt and blue jeans fit well on his slim stature. His demeanor of a scholar was evident as he spoke. "Seeing we're a man down and even though Senator Warren survived, maybe we should contact SIA or one of these superhero groups."

"We went over this before, but I left a message with the secret service, if that makes you feel better." Stargazer replied.

"And?" Master looked annoyed for having to ask more.

"And, if he does his job, he'll report everything I told him.

Hopefully SIA will get the message, which means they'll be looking for us and you need to put something out there that they'll be able to link us to." Stargazer moved the wet clothes onto the floor and leaned back on the cushion.

"Good, because I already made contact with someone who believes us." Master kept a straight face.

All the men looked at the teenager. "What?" Rat Bastard eyed him as if he were left out of a secrecy pack.

"Who?" Stargazer spoke a millisecond afterwards.

"It's a hacker who calls himself Pegasus Prime." Master stood and walked towards the laptops.

The rest of the group followed. "You're going to put our hopes on a hacker?" Spot joked.

"Is it a girl?" Rat Bastard's eyes and smile glittered with joy.

Stargazer also smiled but kept quiet.

"No, it's not a girl. I understand you guys think it could be any person on the planet with no connections, a scammer or be tied to law enforcement. But this guy's different." Master opened up a chat on a website he created.

The log of conversations demonstrated Master's disregard for secrets or social protocol. "You told him that South America would start World War III?" Spot raised his voice of the first time in months.

"We don't know that?" Stargazer chimed in.

"No, but he sure believed me when I started talking about assassins made of metal trying to topple governments."

"Have you seen this guy?"

"Well, yes and no." Master replied. "He gave me the third degree for a while until he realized I'm a genius, and he also confirmed my stories... I also looked into his claims that he could hack into any computer without them knowing it."

"And you believed him?" Spot asked.

"He hacked into NORAD and showed me. So, yeah."

"What if he's with the Chinese or something?" Stargazer retorted with a click of the mouse, closing the window.

"He's with someone, but it isn't China. I have concluded that it's one of the few Super AIs, South America, or Australia... or he's just a one of a kind, authentic badass."

"I assume you covered your tracks." Rat Bastard asked.

"Of course, and so did Pegasus."

"Hmm, well you keep working on it." Stargazer replied then turned towards the adjacent room to shower and change. "Hopefully Ghost will turn up soon."

Several hours passed when Ghost appeared in front of Master while on his laptop. Master jumped out of his seat skipping a few heartbeats. "Aragah! What's wrong with you!"

Ghost smiled. "Sorry Master, I'll knock first, next time."

Three thumps of wood pronounced a real knock on the room's

front door.

"Don't get that." Ghost commanded as Stargazer and Rat Bastard walked into the main room Master and Spot occupied.

"Before you guys go crazy, the guy on the other side of the door is going to help us."

Stargazer looked on the other side of the door. "He's one of the assassins." The men started to move into battle stances.

"He's not going to murder anyone anymore. It's okay, he's on our side." Ghost flew upright through the table, Master and chairs getting in between the group and the front door.

"What's he doing out there?" Rat Bastard asked.

"He's standing there waiting." Stargazer stayed on alert.

"Well show him in then." Rat Bastard cheerfully walked up to open the door.

"I hope you're right." Stargazer said just before Rat Bastard grabbed the door knob.

Ghost concentrated on his friends, seeing their thoughts. The front door opened inward as Io stood with a relaxed posture. "Hello, I'm Io."

"Is he the ninja?" Spot asked noticing that it wasn't the secret service agent they attacked.

"Come on in." Rat Bastard stood to the side, as Ghost also stood to the side to introduce the group.

"Io, who was the imposter agent, this is Rat Bastard, Master, Spot and our leader, Stargazer."

"It is nice to meet you all." Io's voice alluded to a script more than sincerity.

"It sure doesn't sound like it." Spot said as he sat down at the dinette table.

"Excuse the relapse, but my sensors indicate you are unknown alpha class entities." Io looked at Stargazer.

"Yeah, we get that a lot, except for the alpha class." Master sat back down behind his laptops but scrutinized Io as the men conversed.

"I assume you and Ghost have talked about what is going on, so will you care to tell us who and what you are?" Stargazer stood with arms crossed.

Master quickly typed on his laptop, taking an image of Io. Io looked at the laptop's camera and smiled, then walked up and sat down at the table. "Ghost told me you would have these same questions, so I will present the questions and answers. Afterwards, I can answer any new questions you might have. Does that fulfill your expectations?" Io glanced up at Ghost for approval.

Ghost nodded and Io spent several hours informing the group about the Tantalumized androids and Australia's plan to take over major countries before the final stage of world conquest.

The group was amazed to include Ghost who didn't know all the details about the androids' capabilities to impersonate people at will and teleport up to twenty miles every half hour, depending on their ability to accelerate a recharge through a strong electrical power source.

Master confirmed the claim as the facial recognition program told him Io was using the identity of a game store attendant from California.

"If there are so many of you guys, why hasn't Australia taken over the world already?" Rat Bastard asked.

Io looked at him. "There are limitations to our abilities and the initial plan was for a worldwide takeover. However, superhumans are powerful enough to counter the total number of androids created. The failed assassination attempts into South America over the past ten years also caused a mission change into subverting governments and covertly kill as many alpha, beta and gamma class superhumans."

"So you have classifications for superhumans?" Spot said aloud.

"Yes, except for Master, you four are considered alpha class entities."

"So we're the strongest class?" Rat Bastard questionably asked.

"No, beta class superhumans have higher power levels or abilities that can greatly impact events. Gama class superhumans are even more powerful, of eight known gamma class superhumans, seven are currently not on the planet."

"Do you know all of the political and superhuman targets?" Stargazer noted the classifications, but was more concerned if what Cassandra implanted into their memories was accurate.

"Only current US targets."

"And who are they?" Master stopped typing on the keyboard.

Io turned his head and looked at the laptop, interfacing with the wireless connection. A list of twenty-seven names, addresses and bios popped up on the screen. "Those are the remaining targets."

"Senator Warren and Jean Lorenz are still on the list." Stargazer stated seeing the photos and information through the back of the screen.

"Who's Jean Lorenz?" Rat Bastard asked never hearing or knowing about her.

"She's the woman we saved at the airport." Stargazer looked at the rest of the information in thought, trying to figure things out.

"So, it wasn't a total loss." Spot stated.

"It was for a lot of people..." Ghost sadly retorted.

"So how the hell are we going to keep them from trying over and over?" Rat Bastard made fists on top of the edge of the table.

"We lure them together, destroy the androids and put all the targets into a superhuman witness protection program of some kind." Master casually stated as if playing a video game.

"That sounds like a master plan to me." Spot slowly smiled as did the rest of the group except for Io.

Chapter Five

Guild on a Mission

Malleson Estate, New York City

L ee watched the televised assassination attempt on Senator Philip Warren. His sandy blond hair was grown out below his ear lobes. A clear contrast to the military style look of a warrior he had in the past. His blue eyes gazed along the banner as he caressed Diana's shoulder and long red hair.

"Do you think it's one of those machines?"

"It looks like it." Lee held her head in his chest with a hug and kiss.

"Does this mean they will leave us alone?"

"We're too high a profile for now, but I think once they start to succeed, we will see them throw everything they have at us being we'll probably be at the bottom of their to do list."

"We can always disappear and they'll never find us."

Lee turned her face upward so he could look into her hazel green eyes. Diana's body twisted from her side to her back on the linen sofa she laid on. "Do you really want to hide knowing they're going to try to take over the world?" Lee's voice was soft but strong at the same time.

"We can't fight the entire Australian military. Even though you and Mathew might think otherwise." Diana's sweet breath was alluring. Lee didn't know if it was her anti-venom like saliva or her attempt to seduce him into her will.

"Well, no one ever said we would do it alone. But I think we will have to fight them eventually... it might as well be on our terms."

Diana sat up and turned to face her fiancé. "What's going on Lee? We have been trying to get information on them and haven't been able to do anything this past year."

"We have new information and now that Creator has recovered the stealth fighter, we have another objective."

"And when were you going to tell me about this new plan?"

"As soon as I tell Mathew and kiss my goddess." Lee smiled and kissed her for a long while.

The kissing turned into foreplay, until a tall man entered the living room. His dark piercing black hair was cut short, but hinted heavily of Native American linage. "I heard you had something to tell me." Mathew sat on the opposite end of the room. His tie was loose having recently arrived from the office.

"Did you hear that from across the mansion?" Lee asked doubting his own ability to hear things across long distances, having not heard Mathew cross the distance.

"People are selective when they want to be. Like you didn't hear me come into this section of the house."

"No, I heard you, but thought you would at least let us finish what we started." Lee's frown demonstrated a half angry but joking pose.

"Sorry about that, but you made me think. The Bukkang reporting says that the Australians were working on a device to disrupt the atmosphere. So, what if they have more of those things?" Mathew removed his tie and slowly rolled it up with both hands.

"So we find the devices, destroy them or at least tell the superhero groups so they can destroy them." Lee held Diana in his arms and looked at her. "See, our new objective."

"Hmm I like the sound of this plan." Diana admitted and turned her face towards Mathew.

Mathew looked at her with concern. "We aren't going on a killing spree, if that's what you're thinking."

Diana narrowed her eyes. "I love the cloak and dagger stuff too, you know."

Lee smiled. "It's okay Mat. She's turned over a new leaf."

"I never had a problem with you guys killing people, just make sure they're not the good guys." Mathew stood up and started to walk upstairs. "If you do, I'll have to kick your ass."

They watched him leave in wonder. "Do you think he can kick my ass?" Lee asked as Diana rested her head on his lap again.

Diana turned his face towards hers. "You're amazing and all, but I think he can."

"Really? Well I know one thing he can't kick."

"What's that?"

"Well I should say slap." Lee lifted her with his flight power for a second and lightly slapped her butt.

Diana laughed and pushed him back into the sofa and finished what they had started.

Mathew entered his very large master bedroom upstairs on the other side of the four story mansion. Valerie soundly slept under the covers as he eased himself by her side. Her brown hair was coiled up above her head as she turned towards him. She kissed him without opening her eyes.

Mathew returned the kiss and hugged her. "I didn't mean to wake you." He whispered.

Valerie opened her beautiful brown eyes. "Don't you ever crawl into bed without giving me a goodnight's kiss."

"Or, a honey I'm home kiss." Mathew kissed her some more.

They made out and finally slept with new plans set in motion for the group.

The morning came quickly as the entire group met inside of Valerie's office. The panoramic window view of Columbus Park and many buildings towering the great city gave the office a majestic atmosphere. Cynthia and Kyle were the two additions, making the group huddle complete. The six members of the guild with no name sat around the informal conference table as respective couples.

Kyle and Cynthia's marriage ceremony was grand and still seemed to be affecting them many months later with a sparkling fire in their eyes and faces.

Lee and Diana also had a glimmer of shining joy on their faces, but the time had come to get down to business. "Lee and I have talked about how we can use the corporation to bring down the superhuman killers and keep us alive." Mathew spoke aloud not needing to use sign language around the group who knew his true identity.

"Our intel tells us that the Australians helped North Korea create a device to disrupt the Earth's atmosphere. It's likely that as we suspect, so do other people believe that there's more than one of these devices. So we need to find the device or devices and take them out."

"I don't see how or why that's going to stop them from sending more assassins to kill use one by one." Kyle's perfect English reflected his Japanese American appearance and linguist abilities.

"If the devices are taken out, then they will have to start a war to do whatever they had planned on doing. Going around killing superhumans isn't going to work. The Eternal Champions, EFL or South America won't let that happen." Lee stated.

"South America has been neutral for decades. What makes you think they will get involved now?" Cynthia countered as if supporting her husband.

"The Eternal Champions believe that South America is on the verge of starting a war against Australia. They also believe that these mechanical assassins are only a small part of what's to come. So by us destroying these devices before they are used as weapons, will be our contribution." Lee calmly replied.

"Lee's sister works with Creator, so the information is credible." Diana added to the dialogue.

"Really?" Cynthia said while the rest of the group turned towards Diana, having never known Lee's inside source of intel on the Eternal Champions.

"Isis?" Kyle tried to ascertain what sister Diana was referring to.

"No, it's not Isis or Pandora. She's a ghost like us." Lee reported knowing the questions would continue if he didn't give up some ambiguous tidbit of information on Cindy.

"If there aren't any more questions or concerns, I would like to begin our search by back tracking our teams into possible locations." Mathew handed the two couples a folder with satellite and area study documents.

Valerie talked the group through the information in the folders. "The device in North Korea took up an area roughly three square miles given the security zones they set around it. Most of it was underground, but that also limits the locations. Building the device would require a major undertaking which could not just be hidden from a country without its consent or knowledge. This rules out South America, most of Europe and Africa. China is a possibility, but not likely since they are not Australian sympathizers. Of course, there would probably be a device in Australia, but the other ones are the ones we should concern ourselves with."

"So we use our teams to look at the locations in Africa and Europe. We split up and look at Asia and the poles." Lee said as he read the latest updated files on the regions.

"So what do we do once we find one?" Diana's voice was deceptively soothing.

"We wait to see if other regions are cleared. We will take them out all at once if possible." Mathew started to pencil in names to the regions.

"What exactly does this device do?" Kyle looked at the prototype diagram of a particle accelerator type of installation.

"No one really knows, except that it creates a disruptive force field which ionizes air particles, probably to create a hole in the atmosphere.

We think it's some type of global warming weapon." Lee explained.

"Wouldn't that be bad for the Australians too?" Cynthia exclaimed.

"Yes, it would be. Which is why I'm not sure what it really does or how they will negate the effects, but when are weapons of war user-friendly? For now, we go as couples to these areas." Mathew pointed out Antarctica for Lee and Diana, Asia and Europe for Kyle and Cynthia, while Mathew and Valerie would take the African regions for the moment as their recon teams reported back in.

"Won't the Australians be suspicious if we all leave the corporation vacant for weeks on end?" Diana asked.

"We assembled a team to cover for us. They will make sure it seems like we're driving the train. In addition, you will get an update on your projects via a new and secure drop box, so once a week please look at it." Valerie explained.

"We're leaving after work, but you guys can leave sooner if you want." Mathew walked up to the wall-sized window looking out over the city blocks.

The couples in unison stood up, "We'll leave in a few hours." Kyle said and bid everyone goodbye.

Lee and Diana whispered among themselves and also bid the group goodbye. "Lee." Mathew hailed him down as Lee got close to the office's double doors.

Lee turned with Diana by his side, standing at ease.

"Those machines are probably stronger now. If you run into them, do whatever it takes to wipe them out." Mathew said to Lee, but looked at Diana, referring to the first encounter that almost killed

Diana.

Lee smiled and placed a hand on Mathew's shoulder. "I'll wipe out the world to keep her safe."

Diana's eyes tighten along with her jaw. "Don't think I can't take care of myself."

Mathew half smirked. "We all can Diana. But if you guys run into an army of those machines, I would feel better if you let Lee loose and let him do what he does best."

Diana stepped back to put both men in her frontal view. "Is there something both of you are hiding from me?"

Lee stood silent, looking at Mathew. "Lee's powers rival Hellfire's destructive energy output, which he has been keeping a lid on, and I kept quiet until now." Mathew turned his head towards Lee. "I know you have limits, but it's time we go for broke."

"I won't ask how you know, but it doesn't matter... I promise I won't hold back anymore." Lee gripped his hand tighter and let go of Mathew's shoulder in affirmation.

The couple left the office with Diana admiring her fiancé more and more.

Valerie walked up next to Mathew. "It's not like you after so many years of being with you, to keep things from me."

He turned and held her in his arms. "I didn't know. I had a theory and now it's a fact."

Valerie smiled looking deep into his eyes. "Hmm, I love you so much."

"I loved you since the day I caught you red-handed." He smiled and tried to kiss her.

Valerie returned the kiss but spoke as they did. "You were lucky."

Mathew mumbled a response but gave up as they passionately kissed forgetting about the past.

70,000 feet, 200 Miles East of Brazil

Lee's energy suit surrounded Diana as he soared at hypersonic speed southward towards the South Pole. She held tight around his chest, even though he was ensuring she wouldn't fall out of his grasp. Her earpiece and collar microphone worked perfectly as they talked within the energy field as if air turbulence never existed.

"If you keep looking that way for long, you're going to pull a muscle." Diana joked as she every now and lifted her head off his shoulder to see his face.

Lee's helmet visor was clear, but he faced the west instead of forward in the direction of travel. "They scrambled seven fighters in our direction."

"Do you think they can catch us?"

"Not sure, but maybe the ones further south can since they're doing at least Mach 5."

"And we were worried about a stealth fighter falling into the wrong hands."

Lee turned his head at her. His energy armor was very hard, but his superhuman abilities allowed him to change it into any shape or physical attribute he desired around his body. The visor disappeared as did a large section of the front of the black helmet. "As long as we don't pose a threat we should be okay." Lee flew eastward away from the continent, making sure there was no encounter with legendary South American military fighters used in the Caribbean War and takeover of the continent by Colombia.

"I don't know what we would be doing if you hadn't shown up." Diana looked back towards the west seeing a vague line of dark landscape on the horizon.

"Valerie and Cynthia would probably be widows living off the grid and the corporation would be owned by a new puppet." His emotionally empty reply was weird, reflecting his younger self.

"Thank you for not saying the obvious."

"Honestly. I think Mathew would have survived and there would have been a long trail of dead people." Lee caressed her silky red hair.

"Promise me you'll take care of them if I die."

"Stop talking like that. We'll live a long time and have a dozen kids." Lee moved her in a position to be able to have her face to face.

Her frown changed to intrigue. "You can't handle me, what makes you think you can raise twelve rug rats?"

"You keep forgetting we have an army of nannies, three aunts and two uncles who can run a country." His smile melted her heart.

"I won't talk that way ever again."

"You make my life very easy for a goddess." Lee lightly kissed her and then looked westward to confirm the location of the fighters his multidiscipline energy sensors tracked. "They're starting a holding pattern waiting to see if we return near their airspace."

"I thought they couldn't see us on radar." Her eyes narrowed as if wanting to say something else in response to the goddess acolyte.

"Yeah, that bothers me. The only way I can figure is they have a visual on us through satellites or something." Lee sped up and changed course again well over the Atlantic towards Antarctica.

"So how can we lose them?"

"It might be a good thing if they see what we're doing, but I doubt they'll watch us the entire time half way around the world."

"If I had an object flying halfway around the world at extremely high speeds, I would want to track it wherever it went."

Lee half smiled. "Well since you put it that way. Maybe it's good if they do track us. Who knows, they might help us if we run into trouble."

"I hope you're right." Diana placed her head back on his shoulder.

Forty minutes later, the lack of sonic booms didn't diminish the fact of their arrival and the start of a slow aerial recon of the large icy and mountainous continent.

Diana changed position and sat on top of Lee's lower back as they flew close to the ground. Lee's ability to scan twenty square miles all around him didn't keep Diana from having a second set of eyes on the surrounding terrain. After several hours of looking miles inland parallel to the coastline, the couple landed several miles from a Norwegian camp.

"This is going to take forever." Lee said as they stood on a foot of compact snow.

"Don't you think it would be hard to hide such a big contraption out in the middle of nowhere?"

"You would think so, but sometimes it's best to hide something so big in plain sight." Lee scanned the camp seeing people in their routines of surviving and conducting scientific projects.

Diana's white winter ski outfit was more for show than necessity. Both of them could withstand the extreme temperatures far better than any clothing they wore. "Yes, I know they can bury it and cover it up with snow."

"No, I mean they can say it's a radio dish or one of those large buildings." Lee pointed at the image he projected out of his helmet onto the palm of his hand. A large blue two story level building was centered to several other buildings used by the camp as living quarters, a power station and logistical facilities.

"So did we find it already?" Diana stretched her arms behind her head for a brief moment.

"No, it's a normal camp. But if it makes you feel better, they're fully stocked with food. We can get something to go."

Diana's frown turned into a devious smile. "I assume you're providing the heat?"

"Of course." Lee smiled seeing her delight in having to fly underground into one of the pantries and stealing food. "Lucky for us you can ghost us through the ground, while I tell you where to go."

"You're not hungry are you?"

"Neither are you, but I figured we could have some fun... like eating marshmallows on a camping trip."

Diana hugged him as they both turned translucent sinking into the ground. "Okay babe, guide me to the marshmallows." Lee directed her as she used her flight ability to the target ten meters underneath the food storage area. Once inside, Lee's suit provided lighting and effective analysis of prime non-expired goods.

Chapter Six

◆◆◆◆◆

Seeking Answers

1,000 feet above sea level, Andean Region, Eastern Mountain Range, Cali

C aptain, here's the Natal, Brazil report of a hypersonic overpass above the Atlantic." Lieutenant Commander Mora stood wearing a fully black thin layered polycarbon spacesuit awaiting further instructions.

Captain Soto placed the data chip on her wide wristband. The information displayed on a small screen center of the wristband and a holographic display several inches above her hand. Her spacesuit was also black, as were the rest of the Soldiers on the bridge. Her collar however, held three silver circular emblems with a design of the solar system in the middle.

"Thank you Lydia, that's all for now." Captain Soto turned and faced the main screen.

The main screen was broken up into twelve windows displaying live feeds from federation command, the flagship, four area centers covering North America, space operations, naval command, homeland command and three priority activity feeds. Each window had a timer countdown, most being the same, but the latest was on four months eight days and counting.

Soto looked down at her captain's chair console, with all status reports indicating green. She eased back and rested a moment on the head rest. The bridge was moderately lit up almost to a dim, but the long days seemed like they were never dimmed or laminated to optimum intensity. She smiled seeing the crew overseeing the ship's readiness and coordinating support to other ships not ready for launch. The information from Natal was not digitally sent to the bridge, since they were being used as a relay for logistical command and control. She lightly pushed a telescope icon on her console.

"Mister Vasquez, I hope you're monitoring the new reports."

"Affirmative Captain. I also have good news. We have added a possible superhuman alley. I'm sending you their activity in trying to stop the unusual assassination attempts in the United States."

"When did this happen?" Soto tilted her head in curiosity.

"They seem to know Australia's involvement and I haven't been able to completely identify them, but they appeared since the Chicago airport bombing." Vasquez's elderly voice added a sense of wisdom and certainty.

"How long do you think it will be before we have more actionable information on these assassins?"

"Not sure Captain, but I have a feeling this group might help us find a way of neutralizing their effectiveness."

"I'm sure the council will be particularly interested in whatever you come up with." Soto's short black hair was tapered elegantly as she ran a finger through the strands and over her ear. "Councilmember

Estabon personally instructed me to notify them if we come across a solution to the assassins."

"We were there in the room with you Captain." Vasquez's smile was felt through the console speaker.

Soto half smirked. "Yes, Vasquez. I know, which is why I don't care what time it is, if there is anything new, tell me right away." Her level of anxiety was due to the complexity of their mission and grave responsibility in directing special operations in North America.

"Aye aye Captain. You can count on us." He spoke for the entire cyber intelligence operations division.

"Thank you all. Soto out." Her focus returned to reading the new information Vasquez sent her along with the Natal report. The excitement of what would happen in the next few months and extensive leadership training eased her worries a little, seeing the increased worldwide involvement of superhumans in fighting against terror and the pending war with Australia.

The Eternal Domain Battle Room, Octavian Horse Farm

Cindy's golden blonde hair frizzled into many directions as she lifted the cushion away from her face. "What time is it?"

"It's 5:32 am." Erica's seductive echoed voice replied through the ceiling speakers and Cindy's comlink.

Cindy's eyes blinked in and out of drowsiness as she rolled over on her back. The dark ceiling slowly changed to light gray as Erica helped Cindy wake up by brightening the ceiling and walls, but keeping the lights at a low dim. "I don't remember falling asleep."

"You slept soundly for several hours, but it took you a while to enter your REM cycle." Erica's 3D hologram appeared above the black glossy table. "Is there something wrong?"

"A lot of people are going to die, aren't they?" Cindy poignantly rolled back on her side staring at Erica's light green and blue outlined details of a sexy eight inch model of a woman.

"Elizabeth has been wrong before, so you should have more faith in people to do what's right." Erica's eyes had so much detail Cindy could distinguish eye lashes, hair and lip textures, along with the skintight green outfit of one of her favorite Charlie's Angels motorcycle getup.

"Has Richard's gut ever been wrong?" Cindy's gloom turned into a speck of hope.

"Not that I know of, but he hasn't said we would all survive what he suspects."

"You're supposed to cheer me up, not leave me in a pool of dark questions. I have enough of that from everyone else." Cindy managed a half smile of sarcasm.

Erica's head twisted as she thought of a response. For a super AI, she could have answered immediately, but her compassion as a self aware entity, made her pause in a demonstration of empathy. "The human race survives when they need to the most. Cindy, I can't tell you there'll be very little or tremendous amounts of deaths, but if you let fear or worry run your life, it will be painful."

'That's what you call a pep talk?"

"Richard taught me to say it the way it is." Erica placed her interlocked hands down to her front.

Cindy smiled and sat up on the sofa. "Ah, where is Richard now?"

"He's in the danger room running through his warp scenarios."

"Oh, and the rest?"

"They're sleeping of course." Erica crossed her arms.

"Yeah, of course... Arragh," Cindy stretched her arms over her head. "I had the weirdest dream."

Erica stood on the table silently waiting for Cindy to continue.

"There was a group of people in a large warehouse near a harbor or something like it. Actually, there were two or three different groups." Cindy looked down from side to side for a second trying to get the facts straight. "I don't really know for sure, but there was one guy who was going around like some super assassin sneaking up to people and stabling them in the head with some pointed object... but there wasn't any blood."

"That is disturbing, but dreams are sometimes a subconscious idea caused by something you have seen or experienced. Could it be from looking at all those files on recent criminal activity?"

Cindy ran fingers tips through her short hair placing a clip pin claw styling it behind her head. "I don't know... maybe"

"Maybe you just need to take a day off and relax."

"When you guys need me the most?" Cindy crossed her arms and leaned back on the sofa.

"You're no good to the team if you're delirious with workapia."

Cindy sharply narrowed her eyes. "Are you making up words?"

"Working too much is bad for your health, it's a proven fact and since no one wants to give it a name, I call it workapia."

"Tell that to Richard." Cindy joyfully stood up and walked towards the kitchen.

"Richard's health will never be bad due to over working or anything that I know of." Erica etched eyes followed Cindy as her hologram simultaneously appeared inside the battle room kitchen.

Cindy scanned the open room. By no means was the kitchen small or second rate. Four different types of ovens, a walk in freezer, an eight foot island and two pantries was a chef's palace. She opened the refrigerator exposing premade deserts, pastries and left over dinner.

None of the team members needed to eat, except for her and the staff. But she thanked Richard for enjoying the pleasures of tasty food. Her eyes lit up when she found her favorite strawberry delight. "So what's there to do for a relaxing day around here?"

"May I suggest reclining by the pool during the day or maybe taking in a live concert at the university?"

Cindy sat at the island, slowly enjoying her early breakfast snack. "Hmm... That sounds good."

Erica setup her schedule as Cindy finished her snack and headed to her room. A few hours later, Cindy drove through the farm gates towards the early showing of West Side Story at the Broward center for performing arts.

The afternoon brought her back to reclining by the pool. Cindy breathed softly as the Sun warmed her lightly tanned skin. She looked up through the tinted glass tracking a commercial plane high in the sky.

"Hello Cindy." A voice entered her mind.

Cindy's green eyes appeared as she sat up and removed her glasses. "Hello to you too. It's so good of you to answer me when I ask for you."

"I'm sorry; it's been a long two years." Joshua's candid voice reflected his mood which Cindy gladly accepted.

"I miss talking to you, but you already know that." Cindy spoke out loud as if to herself.

"The dream you had was a view into the future." The visions of her dream appeared in her thoughts as if someone were pushing images in front of her eyes.

"Stop that." She strongly blinked with a raised voice. "You can show me that later. I just want to talk for now. But why are you telling me this anyways? Did you put that dream in my head?"

"It's complicated, but yes I put the dream into your head."

Cindy's sighed. "Can you tell me exactly what's going to happen instead of me trying to interpret a dream?"

"You know I do everything for a reason."

"And what possible reason would you have to play mind games with me?"

"If I had just told you what was coming up, you would have never taken in an entertaining play or peacefully relaxing day."

Cindy felt Joshua's calming presence, along with a fatherly self assurance only possible with a... I'm always right attitude. "You could have done that a year ago."

"Yes, but you didn't need it until now."

Cindy laid back down with the glasses on the top of her crown. "Alright, so tell me now what this dream was about."

"The men and women in the warehouse are androids created to kill people to include superhumans. Your team along with others are trying to find out what's going on and stop these mechanical assassins. I could have given Richard this information but you know I always do things for a reason. You need to give him the information, he will do the rest." Details of the dream and added information filled Cindy's memory.

Cindy contemplated what she would tell Richard, but concern filled her heart. "When is all of this dying going to end?"

"The time will soon come when the Earth will go through a transformation. Peace will reign for many centuries and space exploration will provide a means to survive long after the Sun destroys the planet." The story seemed more like a wishful advertisement than reality, but it did ease her morbid view of the future.

"That's my girl. Now, swim a little before you spring the news."

"Thank you, as always." Cindy grinned and dove into the pool with her bright yellow and silver swimsuit.

Chapter Seven

Time Is Against Us

Day 3, Hyatt Regency, Chicago

Senator Warren was moved back into this area and will be staying at the Sheraton." Io announced as he looked outside over the water and DuSable Bridge. The overcast was partly cloudy with rays of sunlight giving a new birth to the city after the hotel attack a few days before.

Spot sat in the living room as the others attempted to form a trap. His task was simple which was to keep an eye on Io. "How do you know that? Can you track everywhere he goes?"

"No, Master has found him through the secure Secret Service channels." Io faced Spot, standing like a statue.

Spot looked down towards the dining table, Master feverishly typing away on two laptops. The free Wi-Fi made many computers easy prey to Io's network sensors. "Well at least we're just a block away."

"Yes, Senator Warren is not in any danger at this time. The probability is high that Adam 214 returned to a linkage location to report the situation. It will be a few hours from now before any other Adams and Eves are tasked to complete the mission."

Stargazer walked over to the sliding window. "How many androids are we looking at?"

Io looked at him. Stargazer knew he had already assessed them as the androids were taught to do. "It will be all of the androids within the surrounding five-hundred kilometers. Twelve in total to be able to defeat three of you, the Senator and a possible additional class A entity. But they will fail."

"We could barely hurt you guys, what makes you think we will do better with a dozen of you?" Spot asked.

"Because there are five of us capable of inflicting disabling damage to all the androids. I know you are concerned with collateral damage, but in order for you to win, you will need to accept losses and use extreme force even if it causes an android to self destruct."

"You sure are showing a lot of compassion for being a self aware machine." Stargazer said what Rat Bastard might have replied with, if he wasn't sleeping in the adjacent room.

"The deaths and suffering caused by their success will exceed any amount of deaths in or around the hotel."

The pointed fact seemed to cut deep, knowing decisions as a leader meant looking at cause and effect and by accepting some degree of potential collateral damage. Stargazer checked his next words carefully before responding; more out of not having to intellectually go back and forth with the AI. "Let's hope you're wrong. But nonetheless, compassion is part of what motivates us, so we take risks when needed."

Stargazer rubbed his chin with a finger while folding his arms on his chest. "You say we have a few hours before they formulate a plan and execute. How did you locate the Senator and decide on when to attack?"

Io sat on the sofa next to Spot. "I infiltrated the ranks a month prior to the execution. Intelligence gathering was the primary objective while we waited for further instructions. The change of orders came three days ago to make it look like an accident. Senator Warren was going to die of a stroke that night; however, your intervention prevented the execution. Adam 214 was backup and must of seen some inconsistent data with a possibility of me being compromised and acted appropriately to complete the mission."

"Would they have any reason to believe you're working against them?" Stargazer sat down across from both men.

"The initial encounter will be in our favor because they will assume I am destroyed; but if any of them get away or transmit an emergency message in the clear, they will initiate countermeasures."

Stargazer leaned forward. "What kind of countermeasures?"

"They will change communication networks, accelerate all missions and kill as many humans as possible before authorities arrive to move on to opportune targets. The attempt is to cause the government to enact Martial law."

Ghost walked in from the kitchenette wide eyed and sat next to Master.

"Why would Martial law be part of the objective?" Master asked from across the floor plan.

Io turned his head looking directly at Master. "All attention will be directed at the United States. Missions internationally will be conducted in a synchronized decisive attack by placing the blame on North Africa."

"Why didn't you guys do that already?" Spot's asked, slack-jawed.

Io turned towards Spot in his usual stolid posture. "We follow orders not asking why, but there are two high probabilities which involve the presence of the Eternal Champions and their ability to uncover plots based on real human thought. Once, telepaths were allowed to perform official investigations, the mission parameters changed. Since Pandora and Mindseye have not been seen in over a year, Command Central changed the parameters once again to slowly topple governments and let them collapse from within. The second scenario is Command Central was not prepared until now to start a world war. Subterfuge by assassination is part of the first phase in such a war."

Ghost moved next to Stargazer. "Remember what I said about acting more emotional?"

Io stared at him and casually relaxed his straight posture. "My apologies, I will use a consistent emotional state instead of running through embedded profiles."

Stargazer rested his elbows on his knees and interlocked his fingers with both hands. "So we have to make sure you're not identified and destroy the androids nationwide. In addition, we have to cut off the source. But first thing is first."

Stargazer turned towards Ghost. "I need you to take the Senator and we need to have a long meeting with him. Then with his cooperation, we talk to SIA and make it seem like the targets have been moved to a centralized location, which Master has already narrowed down to sixteen sites."

"That sounds all neat, but what happens if the androids attack the Senator and find out he's not there?" Rat Bastard opened the adjacent room door.

Stargazer swiveled in his direction. "I'm counting on it. We fight the assassins and take them out. This will more than likely cause them to use all of their androids in North America to converge on the targets. Since by their accounts, they are compromised in losing thirteen androids or if anything, all targets are being moved as a security measure, so attacking the targets with a mass force would be the logical measure before escalating hostilities."

Io eloquently canted his head. "That's an excellent plan."

Everyone stared at him for a moment thinking he had more insight. "I thought so too." Stargazer smiled.

"So when do we get the senator?" Ghost asked.

"Now, that I think about it. We don't, we go to him. Otherwise the security detail will broadcast that he was kidnapped and that's not what we need. I assume the androids have a lot of secret service agent moles."

"There is one in each regional area, but none to fill my position for this region, which means they will use known identities to gain information and replace existing law enforcement personal, or people with access to the target as necessary."

"You mean they will kill people and take their spot." Rat Bastard stated.

"Yes."

"How do you know we're superhumans?" Master asked even though he had no innate super powers besides his intelligence and minute regenerating abilities.

"Our sensors are attuned to identify specific energy levels, density of surface materials and various other bio and physical attributes. However, in most cases, our sensors are not active because it might be detected by certain radar and sonic devices. I didn't know you were a class A entity until I scanned you two nights ago here in this room when we first met." Io spoke to Stargazer.

"Alright, that will work. Ghost, take me and Spot to the Senator." Stargazer stood up and looked at the other three. "You guys wait here until we call you."

Master waved a weak goodbye as he continued to narrow the battleground on his laptops.

"Later." Rat Bastard took Spot's seat.

Stargazer guided Ghost towards the Senator who was in his suite conducting a telephone conference; six agents positioned around the main room carried high tech assault rifles, a standard procedure after the assassination attempt.

Stargazer looked through their clothing and body armor seeing they were not secret service agents, but SIA agents according to the identification on their persons. "SIA is guarding him now. They have depleted rounds and other neat gadgets, but I doubt they'll be able to do anything to the androids."

"Guess they didn't take you seriously about the machine part."

Spot said.

"No, they did. The rounds can probably go through a heavily armored truck... they just don't know how tough they are."

The three flew through the building structure and hovered invisible in front of Senator Warren. The senator sat comfortably with documents spread out on the dining table. A monitor on the table setup for the conference was taking most of his attention. Two assistants on either side helped guide him through the agenda and note taking.

'Okay, we can just appear or we can leave a message before we scare the man a second time.' Stargazer thought as Ghost relayed the message among the men.

'Well the message as a warning worked better the last time we did something like this. So do we use the keyboard again?' Spot asked.

Ghost flew up guiding the other two just above the keyboard. 'Okay one of you type in a message.'

Stargazer reached out with a hand and started typing after opening a blank word document. [Senator, this is your protectors. I beef you to tell the guards to be calm and not report anything. We are in front of you and need to talk so people won't die.]

'Beef? and...' Ghost started to ask.

'It's not easy typing upside down.' Stargazer interrupted.

The three looked at the message then one of the assistants stood up.

"Please don't be alarmed, we're here to help, so please sit down." Stargazer spoke loud enough for only the three to hear and anyone else on the other end of the microphone.

The elderly senator quickly grabbed the assistant's wrist. "It's okay Kevin. Sit down." Warren's initial alarm faded quickly as he thought about how he was saved two days ago. "I'm guessing you're the real deal by warning us about you, otherwise we would already be dead." Warren looked across at the lead SIA agent.

"Agent Dash, we need to talk right now." Warren turned off the conference and waited for the agent.

Agent Dash rapidly walked up to the table. "Are you done with the conference Sir?" His tall and very muscular stature was notable even under the specialized flexible body armor.

"Don't be alarmed. We have company and your guards need to treat them as friendly. I'm assuming your boss needs to be called immediately so we can discuss what our new friends have to say."

Dash's sanguine demeanor changed to alertness. "What company?"

"Right next to you. But please tell your agents not to go Rambo on us and act like we're supposed to be here." Stargazer instructed.

Dash looked at empty air and then around toward his men. He paused a moment in thought before speaking. "Agents do not raise your weapons, this is a code 48." The agents in line of sight and over the internal ear sets acknowledged.

"They have a code for this?" Spot asked surprised.

"Yeah, how many invisible superhumans are there?" Ghost added.

"Three that we know of, but you're number four or six." Dash faced the direction of the voices.

Ghost, Stargazer and Spot appeared between the dining table and living room, a short distance from Dash. The three were dressed in suits similar to the Secret Service agents, but Ghost and Spot needed a good shaving before they would be mistaken for federal professionals.

The Senator left the table to greet the men as the surrounding guards faced the group. Their weapons were pointing down, but Stargazer knew they were ready with chambered rounds at anytime to start a firefight.

"Senator, I'm Stargazer, this is Spot and this is Ghost." The men shook hands while Dash stayed close to Warren's side.

"I don't know what to say except to ask you if you're the ones who saved me two days ago."

"Yes, it was. And as you know by now, these assassins are not going to stop until you or they are dead." Stargazer slowly walked around the sofa to take a seat, motioning everyone else to rally around the living room table.

Warren breathed heavy as the reality weighed on him. "I know I ruffle some feathers around Capitol Hill every once in a while, but what did I do to deserve the death penalty?"

The trio watched the old man sit with difficulty and a picturesque smile trying to joke his fear away. "Don't ask me how we know, but you need to get your boss on the line along with the Eternal Champions, because there are hundreds of these killer androids worldwide. We came to you because there is a high probably they will return in numbers to finish the job." Stargazer looked back and forth between Senator Warren and Dash.

Dash quickly spoke into his comlink a second time. "This is Lt. Dash authentication 3902231Foxtrott, I need a direct line to Max; Priority alpha one." The comlink on his wrist displayed a small video of an operator on the other end.

"I hope that's secure, otherwise the bad guys will know the gig is up and we can't trap them." Stargazer stared at Dash.

"It's as secure as it can be, unless we go to SIA headquarters which will take an hour at best from here."

"Okay, we'll go and take the Senator. Make sure his plans are changed and he is evacuated to a location…" Stargazer paused waiting for Ghost to fill in the blank.

"There's an abandoned installation along Lake Ontario in Henderson, New York. We need people to think the Senator was moved there for the moment. In the meantime, we will fly the Senator and you to SIA headquarters. There're three others with us and we all need to get there without alerting possible moles in the Treasury Department to include local police. The assassins can impersonate almost any human or same size objects, but we can see them without too much difficulty so everyone should be safe around us. Okay, I got to go and get the other three." Ghost hastily explained reading Stargazer's plan and flew off disappearing before making contact with the ceiling.

"When he gets back, we'll be able to go to SIA headquarters in less than twenty minutes, so just tell them to be ready with a package of eight people." Stargazer stood up looking around the room. "These agents need to clear the area taking the assistants with them. No one sticks around after we're gone, otherwise the assassins might come here and find out that we're involved and that they're compromised. This will start a rampage of terror, so I assume your guys can handle this?" Stargazer faced Dash.

Dash nodded, spouting instructions to his men, as they quickly jumped into sterilization protocol getting all of the Senator's and staff's personal items evacuated along with the assistants.

Spot stood up ready for the flight to come, watching the men meticulously and rapidly gather any evidence of the occupants not vacating properly.

Ghost appeared with Rat Bastard and Master several minutes later. Io teleported next to them inside the now crowding penthouse. Everyone stopped working for a brief moment with a startled reaction, but commenced once the vision of Rat Bastard's giant like stature faded with an urgency to finish packing.

"How are we going to do this?" Master asked, sporting a large tan heavy cloth backpack, a computer cord hanging out of a partially zipped side pocket.

"Spot you take Io and Rat Bastard. Ghost will make sure Agent Dash, Master and the Senator don't die while I fly them to SIA headquarters." Stargazer moved next to Master, pushing the cord into the cloth pocket and zipping it close.

Senator Warren returned with a small carry on sized bag, stopping in the middle of the men. "I'm not sure how all this works, but I trust we won't die on our trip."

"Teleport to the roof, Rat and I will meet you there." Spot said after walking up to Io and then turned to Ghost.

"It's simple. You stand here and here." Stargazer pointed and directed Dash, Warren and Master to stand evenly separated around Ghost and himself. "When everyone is ready, Ghost and I will hold your wrists. That way you can't accidently let go or get tired as I fly us through the building and to SIA headquarters. Senator, I wish there was an easier way but time is against us." Stargazer said, seeing anxious faces after he said through the building."

"Senator?" Dash gave the man an encouraging look.

Senator Warren swung the bag over his shoulder managing a

brave smile. "I have always wanted to know what all the hoopla was about."

"Oh you will like it a lot." Rat Bastard smiled for everyone.

Stargazer looked at Dash and extended his hands out for people to start to get into the formation he designated. "Ready?"

Dash turned his head toward one of his men. "Make sure you're gone in ten."

The agent held several pieces of luggage filled more with equipment than clothing. "On our way out, Sir."

Ghost gripped the two people next to him, making the group intangible. Spot and Rat Bastard were included in the count until they flew up through the building, getting dropped off with Io.

The spectral essence of their bodies was amazingly breathtaking for Dash and Warren. They could see the group members as if all of them were phantoms made of several different tints of silver and white. However, the rest of the world was naturally saturated in respective hues.

"Holy cow! This is…" Warren's bewilderment turned to fearful excitement as Stargazer bolted the group into silent hypersonic speeds soaring over the cloud cover with ease far from the city.

"Holy crap." Dash muttered over his shoulder seeing what many astronauts enjoyed while nearing outer space.

"Yeah, that sums it all up." Master's amusing grin was felt; Ghost making it possible for the group to communicate.

Chapter Eight

Very Nice

<u>SIA Headquarters, New York</u>

Acompany of agents and Soldiers scrambled along the main entrance with anticipation of the unknown superhumans. The high alert around the installation was intense as if they were already under Martial law. Full body armor and heavy weaponry was clearly being used to protect the installation, in addition to air defense and armor assets all around the 6,000 acre property.

"Well I hope your people listen to you. They seem to have a brigade of Soldiers running around expecting an attack." Stargazer fixed his eyes on Dash.

"It's standard procedure with inbound unknown superhumans. I will need to report to the security commander before we're allowed to enter. But how do you know they're fortifying?"

"I can see them from here. Normally we would just fly through all that stuff and appear in front of your boss, but due to the current situation, we'll use the front door." The group's re-entry into the air space wasn't detected by anyone as Ghost made sure the group was invisible, but Dash's awe could be felt among them.

The bunker entrance was wide enough for ten people side by side with four double doors in normal use, but now only one door was active. The chain of security points, fire lanes and choke points made the place extremely suited for aggressive defensive operations, but there was something else that made it formidable against most superhumans. An energy field within the inner primary section of the base seemed like it was surrounded by a few hundred transformers. Stargazer smiled as he slowed down to three hundred meters out and slowly landed the group twenty feet away from a line of Soldiers standing in plain view.

"Okay, I will introduce myself before we appear in front of them. If there's an itchy trigger, I don't want one of you guys to get a bullet." Stargazer forced the Senator and dash to hold hands while he let go of their wrists.

Stargazer appeared in full view of the Soldiers with his two piece suit. He ran a finger along his collar then straightened his tie as the Soldiers went into full warning mode. Seven laser dots appeared on his chest and head, as they shouted commands.

"I'm one of your arrivals. Agent Dash and Senator Warren will appear next to me so please don't shoot and please lower your weapons."

The Soldiers continued aiming at Stargazer, but the instant appearance of the group a few meters to his side partially startled them, but their training kept them from firing a round.

"I'm agent Kevin Dash, authentication HD19V210." Dash slowly raised his hands.

"Lower your weapons." The squad leader ordered and spoke into his helmet mic tapping the side of his visor. "Agent Dash and his entourage are at the main entrance now. Call up the commander and inform Max."

"There are three more on their way, but you'll know when the…" Multiple sonic booms overhead interrupted Stargazer. The ground shook for a second, as he scanned the area. All of the windows in the county were constructed to specs able to withstand such shockwaves. It was apparent sonic booms were common around the base causing Stargazer to admire the public's response to superhuman antics.

Spot, with Rat Bastard on his back as the Rat and Io next by his side impacted against the concrete instead of landing, leaving a chipped impression of two pairs of feet. Rat let go of his grasp on Spot and reverted back to human form lightly standing next to him. Instead of looking around like the other two, Spot reached down and felt the flatten soles of his destroyed dress shoes. "Damn it."

Io turned his head to him glancing at the shoes. "You can probably find another pair inside the installation."

Spot sighed, fragments of the heels laid on the pavement. "I miss my sniper suit."

Stargazer walked up to them. "Io, please don't say anything until I introduce you properly."

Io turned to him with an attentive look. "Understood."

The group waited patiently for the commander and permission to enter the headquarters. Rat Bastard and Master seemed to be the most excited about the visit. It wasn't long before the entire group was in a large conference room attached to a situation command center. The one way windows allowed all members to see out into the center, which seemed to diminish the sense of security for classified information. But Stargazer knew full well they were very secure and at liberty to say what they needed to say. There were no signs of any androids within sixty miles of the headquarters, except for Io. So, when Max entered with his team of experts, everyone thought the meeting would begin.

Everyone had body armor on, the guards with headgear locked into position, while the experts sat around the large table accommodating twenty seats, with additional seating along the side walls.

"Good afternoon everyone." Max greeted, with a hand shake first with Stargazer. "I've been waiting a long time Mr. Messer."

Stargazer smiled. "You wouldn't believe me if I said it has only been months for me."

Max's gray eyebrows lightly lifted. "I've come to believe impossible is a relative word." He said as everyone sat in their assigned seats.

"Good to know we agree on something already... So is everyone here?" Stargazer asked, seeing two reserved empty chairs on the other side of Max.

Ghost looked around uneasy. Creator and Night appeared in front of the turned off display screen facing the rectangular table. Both men were tall, equal to Stargazer; Night being slender, covered in complete black and blue lightning bolts around his wrists extending to the chest and down to the feet. Creator's shades disappeared sinking into his face, leaving his trade mark pointed ears and black eyeballs in clear view.

Most of the people in the room were alarmed even though many had experienced Creator's instant dramatic entrance in the past. Stargazer was also impressed, having not seen them with his vision, as if they had the same powers Ghost so offend used with impunity.

"Well, it seems you're really not the only ghost around." Rat Bastard whispered.

"Mr. Messer" Max began the introductions.

"Stargazer or Steve, if I may correct you?" Stargazer started to stand, but Creator extended his hand before he could and continued on to the rest of the group.

"Stargazer it shall be, and..." The greetings were exchanged with Creator scrutinizing Io the most. "Okay, what's going on?" He kicked the meeting off as if he owned the place.

"There's someone else here." Ghost warned.

"Really?" Creator quickly replied. "Who?"

Ghost felt a little uncomfortable by his gaze as if looking into a dark abyss, but yet somehow feeling a sense of security wanting him to be fighting by your side. "I think it's... a woman."

"Huh, it's okay, she's with us. Her name is Mirage."

Max turned a stare at Creator. Ghost saw a glimpse of what Max was thinking in surprise, before a mental block was forced into his head. "You also have telepathic people in this room."

"Yes, there are two telepaths here to keep others from mentally probing people." Max motioned to the two guards by the door.

"Standard protocol, even though our minds are guarded, but I'm sure they're trying to figure out why they can't sense Mirage, yet you can; but anyways, we're not here to compare abilities." Creator looked at Ghost and Max, then at Stargazer.

"Agree. Bottom line is Australia has created Tantalumized androids made of a form of nano-technology with the ability to teleport, use superhuman like powers, change into any human form at will and each are self-aware with the processing speed of an artificial intelligence. Their plan is to disrupt the stability of governments before trying to take over the world. But, I have a counter plan. First, you need to know the threat better before I go over it." Stargazer looked around into everyone's eyes as he spoke. "Io here is living proof about these androids and he will brief you about them. Io, please explain to them what we discussed in a short version of twenty minutes or less."

"Do not be alarmed ladies and gentlemen. I am one of thirteen thousand eight-hundred thirty-two active Tantalumized beings." Io watched the reaction of the new audience seeing more intense interest than surprise or fear.

Io expertly relayed all information about the Australian objectives and android specifics. The five SIA experts, three superheroes and Erica stayed quiet at the end of the briefing. "Before we go any further, should we inform EFL?" Max turned towards Creator.

"Erica, please relay the information to them."

"Relaying now." Erica's echoed voice came from Creator's comlink.

"What's the plan?" Creator urged Stargazer to continue instead of waiting for EFL to reply.

"We have a list of targets that we need to get into hiding. Io knows the moles and who we can fool into believing they all have been moved to this installation." Stargazer pointed at Master's laptop displaying a satellite image of an abandoned military installation.

"The androids do have weaknesses we can exploit, but we six can't do it alone. Having a group of agents would be nice, but that will only put your agents in harm's way for no reason. We don't know any superhumans able to help out, so we came here. Not to mention to save

Senator Warren's life a second time." Stargazer looked at Max and Creator for a response.

"EFL and Night can help keep the androids from escaping. Mirage and I can help in the ambush area. I assume you picked the location because you expect one or more of them to explode?" Creator gave Max a passing glance now knowing the real cause of the airport explosion in Chicago.

"You anticipate a dozen androids. How are we going to destroy the other thirteen thousand plus?" Cindy's voice originated from above and behind Creator.

Stargazer focused his vision in the few cubic feet behind Creator, seeing only molecules of air particles and minute bits of dust from the air conditioner. "That's a little bit more complicated, but it will involve more outside help. But for now we need to focus on this plan; the only problem I can foresee is the installation needs to look like it's housing the targets. They will expect security and according to Io, it might be possible for Ghost, Io and you to be the bait." He diverted his gaze on Creator. "They don't know about Ghost's existence or Io's new allegiance. I heard you're a shape shifter, but not sure if they will be able to identify you from long range. Unless, you guys have a better idea?"

Creator smiled and transformed, duplicating Io down to the minute essence, even his voice. "I can come close enough."

"Nice." Master said under his breath.

"Yeah, nice." Stargazer agreed, seeing the molecular structure of Io almost duplicated perfectly, even giving him the dense metallic appearance.

"Don't we have a timeline to meet? We don't want to miss our own trap." Rat Bastard asked hoping to end the meeting.

"Okay, we make the rest of the coordination on the way. Erica will confirm the plan. I do have a concern for Master, so may I recommend he stay with Erica or Bob?" Creator stood up.

"Really?" Max raised his eyebrows.

"Master can work out of my headquarters a lot better than here, plus he'll have crazy fast internet."

"How fast?" Master's mouth was watering.

"As fast as any device can handle."

Master rapidly turned his head towards Stargazer in anticipation. "Yes, you can go with them." Stargazer caringly smiled.

"Very nice." Master's awed grin followed him as Night grabbed his arm and they both turned invisible a second later.

Creator turned back into his superhero appearance and stood in front of the blank display screen. "I know you have to report things up to the President, but I think we need to hold off any information past this room and command center until after we destroy these androids. Any leak needs to be controlled and the less people that know, the better."

"Just like in North Korea, so let's make it happen, people." Max reiterated looking all around the room.

Creator smiled as Rat Bastard spoke. "What happened in Korea?"

Chapter Nine

No Survivors

C hiling wind carried large ice particles brutally beating the frozen landscape. Blistering below zero temperature kept wildlife away from the barren area as Lee and Diana slowly flew above along a systematic route. The several days of surveying mostly empty ground was tedious even though they were used to casing people and sites for weeks on end.

"Whoa!" Lee suddenly swooped upward and stopped mid air staring into the darkness of gusting snow.

"What is it?" Diana concentrated her stare in the direction of travel.

"I don't know, but it's huge." Lee looked up and to the sides trying to measure the anomaly.

"Where is it?"

"It's about twenty feet in front of us. It looks like an energy field of some kind. Maybe a cloaking field." Analysis data popped up inside of Lee's helmet indicating incomplete information and unknown light refractions. "Let me try something, but I need you to phase us so we can go underground."

Diana phased them both as they flew straight down into the ground. Lee magnified his modified x-ray vision to penetrate the ice and rock as far as possible. "Wow..." Lee guided them deeper into the ground and moved closer to the target. "You're not going to believe this." His voice was clear within Diana's phased state and his energy suit's internal comms.

They floated up and stood on leveled ground on the other side of the field. The ground was cool and rocky dark. Diana twirled around seeing the inside of a dome like shape of dark white snow several miles wide. The blowing wind was mild as if the energy field directed the harsh environment towards some other dimension. "What the hell? How's this possible?" She looked to the rising terrain in the center and city like structure surrounded by a long rock salt looking wall similar to a defensive perimeter against a ground assault in some fantasy game.

"Stay phased." Lee warned. "They might see us if we go into the physical world." He could make out over two dozen androids and another two dozen humans. "They might still be able to see us now." He floated them back down; hiding their bodies with only their nose on up sticking out of the ground.

"It's bigger than the diagrams."

"It's three times as big as the schematics we saw and with modifications it seems. Most of it is underground."

"Maybe that's how they can generate so much power for this cloaking field?"

"Yeah, well I don't think they made it."

"Are you saying its alien?"

Lee faced her as they held hands underground. "Most likely, the scary version of aliens. We need to get the others and return. I have the layout and personnel information now, so this shouldn't be too hard."

"Lead the way." Diana let him fly the path back under the energy field which extended ten meters into ice and earth.

Lee slowly flew out a hundred meters underground as much as Diana could handle to make sure they cleared the area. Once above ground, they flew at low level passing Mach 2 for thirty minutes before arriving at an American base camp and transmitting the information to rest of the guild.

The camp was not as touristy as the Norwegian scientific site, but it was large with half of the occupants out on expeditionary mapping and study. The couple waited on recliners inside one of the vacant entertainment rooms. Lee's energy suit was gone, but his active radar kept someone from accidently walking in on them. An hour passed before Mathew called them back. Lee put the call through on speaker phone, his glasses facilitating the communication as it was the focal source of his helmet.

"We're on our way, be there in an hour." The text read and sounded, minimizing long transmissions and traceable information.

Lee projected the image of the installation on the back of one of the several rows of recliners. They spent the hour going over the information and coming up with courses of actions.

The faint sonic booms they heard were very high and far from them, completely unheard by normal human ears, but it signaled the arrival of the team.

It wasn't long before Kyle appeared in front of them as Sia. His ninja black outfit was a little deceptive since his hands were gloved, had boots and the belt around his waist was more a utility device with thin boxes and snaps. Mathew, Valerie and Cynthia quickly appeared next to him as if their bodies were ant size, transforming to normal height in less than a second. All three were in uniform as Hawk, Hummel and Evergreen. Mathew had black goggles and a holstered side pistol resembling a laser with an artillery muzzle. The black outfit was similar for all three except his right arm and hand were red. Valerie's hair was wrapped in a pony tail, while Cynthia's hair freely draped down her back. The goggles the women wore seemed to be enough disguise for their liking. More a non-formality since their existence was a closely guarded secret and their execution of missions almost never attracted attention or offered up opportunities for witnesses.

Valerie put forth an empty palm facing upward. A goggle with a head strap expanded out to medium size. "This is for you D."

"Thank you V."

Lee's suit appeared all around him, his entire body was like a black phantom with cornered edges. "I like it when you guys talk in brevities."

Mathew smiled, but only Lee saw it being able to see through their uniforms. "Maybe we should use the letters instead of our long names."

"Yeah, V sounds better than Hummel."

"I'll keep Sia if you don't mind." Kyle objected as he shook Lee's hand along with a man hug.

"Yeah, you don't look like MIB material." Mathew grinned as Valerie made everyone except Lee as small as an ant. A hole opened up on Lee's suit above his heart. The group flew inside his protective energy suit and down his shirt front pocket. Lee walked up outside of the building, "Is everyone settled in?"

"We're fine; just don't go digging for a pen or something." Diana replied.

"You're lucky I don't carry a nerdy calculator." Lee flew into the darkening sky leaving at Mach 2 without a sound.

Shortly afterwards, Lee landed just outside the energy field, everyone exiting his pocket.

The attack plan was set into motion as the six superhumans traveled underneath the energy field all the way to the main structure.

An array of consoles with monitors and buttons displayed the atom accelerators as working within acceptable parameters. Five men sat and stood in the upper level fifty by fifty foot control center.

A technician walked from one section to another with a tablet going down a checklist. He coughed softly to pause for a moment. The immediate irritation in his face increased as his persistent cough turned into a suffocating choke. He vainly ripped away at his shirt collar, grabbing his throat as he fell on his knees, then his face. The other men looked at him with fear or surprise.

The first man to come to the technician's aid also fell in similar fashion. No matter the distance from the fallen comrades, all five breathed their last in a span of seconds, their skin turning a black and red pigment as cells quickly died. Kyle and Diana appeared in front of the center console with Kyle reading the information and switching a few dials as if he knew the controls. "Do you know what you're doing?" Diana asked.

"I don't have a PhD in computer science for nothing." He flipped through a technical manual on the counter space.

Diana looked at the monitors and decaying flesh of what used to be men. "I think you need more like a physics or nuclear degree."

Kyle narrowed his eyebrows as the complexity of the displays revealed more than connecting networks of data batches and commands. "Maybe Cynthia should have come with us."

"She wouldn't know what to do either." Diana walked over to the main door.

"Okay, guys, we're in position." Kyle said, tapping a button on the side of his belt.

"Lee, go ahead." Mathew came over the secure transmission with all people ready to destroy the enormous device instead of waiting to find possible other options.

Lee scanned several large car sized severs in the upper story of the device. Two men lay on the composite floor dead, with gaping cauterized burnt holes in their heads. Lee's armor extended beyond the centimeter barrier around his hand and into the data cables.

Petabytes of data downloaded into his storage interface. "Damn, there's a lot of information in these things."

A ninety-two percent capacity readout of his storage limit came up in front of his eyes within his helmet. "Hmm…" Lee paused the download and focused on his communication configuration located in his necklace. His long-range communication files dumped and all of the new information was drastically compressed. In a few minutes, he completed the download of close to five Exabytes of data.

"Okay, all done."

"It's about time, did you lose your touch?" Valerie asked.

"Heads up. They're on to our transmissions." Mathew said.

Lee looked at the android locations and patrol routes. Half of them inside the complex itself were not in their previous locations. He looked through the area seeing three androids teleporting through the device room by room. "Okay, plan A as expected."

Mathew and Valerie disappeared from their location at one of the power transformer rooms.

Kyle and Diana also vanished as quickly as they appeared; the consoles all damaged beyond repair by a sharp swipe of Kyle's deadly hands and feet throughout the entire room.

Cynthia stayed quiet outside on top of the tallest structure of the complex.

Lee turned towards the center and down where the inner energy cylinder was extending as far as he could see; several hundred meters straight down. He extended his hand out to his front. A barrel protruded out of his armor above his forearm.

Blinding laser light pulsed out melting everything in its path. It hit the energy field only to disperse the energy without penetrating it. Lee swirled his aim creating a four foot wide arched hole all the way from his location to the center cylinder shaped force field protecting the core of the device.

A stocky man in white camouflage winter apparel teleported inside the room. Lee twirled around lasing the man in the neck and head with lightning speed. The android's head dropped to the floor, rolling several times as the rest of his body flopped heavily on a wheeled chair, crushing it into submission. Lee's sensors tracked six androids within four room's distance. He dove through the hole, flying at top speed next to the inner force field, then out of a direct line of sight from where he left the neutralized android.

Four quick glimpses of men teleporting into the room and then teleporting out after Lee could barely be noticed, except by the air vibrations in the room along with one of the sever boxes cracking due to the proximity of the teleportation field.

The open area of space straight down and up existed between the long corridor containing the center accelerator and hundreds of levels of the device. However, Lee had very little to move around side to side which extremely hampered his flying power. As soon as he turned around to face the exit of the hole he created, the four androids were already in the thirty foot wide by nine hundred meter deep empty space.

Lee looked left and right, reassessing his decision to enter inside the accelerator's casing. His sensors indicated an energy source in the center, but he couldn't tell if it was the force field around it, or if there was something else inside the fifty meter barrel like cylinder. He flew straight down to get some distance from the androids as he fired up with his lasers coming out of both forearms.

To his surprise, he missed one android and the others sustained major damage to an arm or leg, but persisted in their pursuit slightly behind the unharmed android. Lee saw projectiles leave two of androids' hands. The round like objects sped at him at supersonic speed causing muffled sonic booms inside the chamber. Lee's reflexive response was mirrored by the androids as he barely dodged five rounds that either penetrated the shell outwards into the ground or inward into the force field cylinder.

Lee's sensors told him they were no longer in the central portion of the device, but were heading deeper into the Earth's crust. His helmet allowed him to see in the very dark environment with an aura of light coming from the light green force field surrounding the accelerator and his almost white laser beams. He looked at the bottom reach of the accelerator with concern as it ran a good two miles before it seemed to come close to the upper mantle.

Steel like hands grabbed his upper arms from behind as he soared downward. The energy armor held strong as the pressure increased to metal crushing intensity. Lee strained to twirl around only to force the android to stay on his back. Another android teleported in front of Lee and fired two rounds from the inside of his hands. The point blank attack ensured a hit, but the titanium rounds mushroomed and bounded back on the android's hands. The android looked at the slight damage of the rounds to the surface of his skin with surprise.

Lee's data feed on his armor showed a weakening of the armor for a fraction of a second where the rounds hit, but it was instantly reinforced by redistributing his energy evenly around his body. The other two androids held back by ten meters as two laser beams came out of Lee's palms aimed towards his back and front.

The point blank position of the androids worked both ways and the both androids were cut in half just below the waistline.

Lee expected the android at his back to let go of his arms, but instead the android exploded into a ball of disintegrating energy. The essence of Lee's armor held strong, as it absorbed or redirected a good portion of the deadly reaction. The second android also exploded as if he were a domino made of the same volatile properties.

The shockwave reached the surface, as Lee skimmed along the

cylinder's force field. The implosion of rock would have been greater had the explosions not instantly baked large spherically shaped melted or harden surfaces around where the androids exploded. Lee tracked the two unharmed androids several hundred meters up having moved out of the kill zone, as two other androids joined the battle. The impact of his armor with the inner cylinder force field took most of his attention. The green energy caused multiple alerts to pop up in his visor as the energy was damaging the points of contact on his armor a lot more than anything he had encountered in the past.

Lee focused on stabilizing his body and armor being linked to his superhuman abilities. The armor regenerated instantly as expected, but it took time which the androids noticed. As Lee recovered into a leveled flight path from the explosive push an android teleported next to him. The android's arm jackknifed as it made contact with Lee's side as he countered the attack with a split second of flight.

The attempt to send Lee into the force field helped him take the android's arm and flip him into the energy shield. A laser beam hit the android center mass as Lee with an extended hand flew up at the three androids. The anticipated explosion occurred on cue while the androids hovered in mid air. A mixture of attacks came out of the machines directed at Lee. The metallic projectiles and radiated pulse beams hit numerous areas of his body inflicting minor damage. The lightning bolt coming from one of the androids actually helped energize his armor.

The laser cannons on Lee's forearms retracted as if evaporating at the same time, but the thousands of laser beams coming out of his entire body were no less powerful or deadly at short range. The attack caught the androids by surprise as they received catastrophic damage. Thousands of nickel size fifty meter deep holes in the rocky background were replaced by the three synchronized explosions.

The earth shook violently as the combined concussive effects hit

Lee with fantastic strength. Gravity took control as heavy rock and minerals caved inward along the vertical energy cylinder and on top of Lee. His penetrating radar looked out to a limiting thousand meters through rock, which was the problem. The once small opening he could see straight up was replaced by darkness.

Above ground, androids rushed around searching rooms and securing critical areas only to find four areas already compromised. Human workers ran into safe rooms as part of lockdown procedures. Mathew jumped from one structure to another shooting his pistol at any opportune target. If it wasn't an android or human, it was security cameras, antennas, exposed cabling or doors. The energy blasts from his pistol acted like small tank rounds with extreme knockback properties. He super leaped to the top of structures and down into alleyways making himself hard to hit as androids pursued and fired at him with large mini-guns under their arms.

The projectiles hit hard on Mathew's back and legs, but with his density increased, the rounds only altered his direction of travel. He awkwardly recovered his landings and had to kick off of walls to continue the momentum. A trail of thousands of fist size holes followed Mathew's route. He smiled as the constant salvoes by the androids helped in destroying the complex.

He looked at his last destination, sensing thirty-two androids hot on his heels and to his front. The clearing he was hoping to reach, came a little short as two strong energy beams hit him from behind. The heat was bearable, but it would have instantly burnt through a whale, unlike his skin leaving only two burnt holes on his uniform. His boots sank a few inches into the hard rocky ground as he swiveled around facing the majority of the androids and laser attacks.

He listened to his keen senses and as if grabbing an invisible tube he reached out with both hands. An android teleported to his side, Mathew instantly held his wrist, braced back with a foot and swung up and over with all his strength. The six foot android lifted off the ground and was flipped to the opposite side, body slamming into another android trying to grab Mathew from both sides. The ground gave way to both androids as if two metal drills buried themselves several feet into the earth. As quickly as he downed the androids, three others teleported and jumped on top of Mathew.

Mathew's quick draw made one sounding shoot but three energy rounds came out. Each android received an energy round in the chest, penetrating their Tantalumized exoskeleton by an inch. The damage was not severe, the cavity refilling itself within seconds, but the knockback of the rounds pushed the androids away from Mathew twenty meters. Mathew twirled around three times, firing as fast as possible all around him. The blasts were somewhat sporadic hitting android and structures without effective precision.

All the androids came within meters of Mathew ready to pounce on him, knowing he would not be able to out power them or escape. One android facing Mathew looked up into the sky detecting a flying object. Wide bright green energy blasts spread out covering the one hundred meter square area around Mathew.

Cynthia's gamma particle attack hit all of the androids, but they didn't disintegrate or melt the android's unusual alloy. One android lost a leg, but didn't explode as the others. Mathew, Cynthia and Valerie looked on as one android exploded and the others teleported out of the path of destruction as if they were interlinked with a reflexive or automated program to move to safety once an android self-destructed.

"Protect Evergreen!" Mathew yelled as he leaped at one of the androids closest to the Cynthia who was high in the air.

Eight androids teleported two hundred meters up next to Cynthia. She started to fly at hyper speed, but six titanium rounds from the multiple android miniguns hit her all over her body.

Cynthia's arm, chest, legs and hip ached in pain as the rounds partially penetrated her flesh, causing her to stop flying at maximum speed; her momentum keeping her in the air, moving eastward. An android teleported above her and thrust a fist into the back of her head. His knuckles hit hard, but not at the same speed as the titanium rounds. Cynthia's body followed her head downward as she instantly shrunk out of sight. The androids looked at Cynthia's last location, following their scan to Cynthia being carried by Valerie back down on the ground. Her miniaturized state was difficult to track, but not impossible as a nearby android shot a blot of electricity in their direction. The electrical bolt danced along the ground and significantly diminished in power as it shrunk into a small static spark.

Mathew grappled an android yanking off his head with great difficulty only to be at ground zero of the self-destruct measure. The energy pushed him away a few feet as if he were almost immoveable, with most of his outer uniform being shredded to pieces.

Mathew stood at the ready with pistol out in one hand. The androids repositioned themselves around him and Valerie. A smile came over him as white laser beams hit all of the androids slicing them in half, leaving very deep trenches and holes in the ground.

All but two androids exploded leaving many twenty meter diameter craters and rock fragments imbedded into concrete walls towards the base structures. Lee hovered above the center of the complex half a mile away. Cynthia appeared next to Mathew. Malformed titanium, warheads seemed to instantly grow outside of her wounds as if something was spitting them out.

Kyle and Diana appeared next to them as the last round was ejected out of Cynthia's body. "Sorry we couldn't help in time." Diana said.

"It's okay you and Kyle would have been hurt badly if you entered the crossfire." Mathew replied.

Kyle took Cynthia into his arms, relieving Mathew from the task of holding her in a sitting position. "Now I know not to let them hit me." Cynthia moaned a little as her body slowly regenerated muscle and skin.

Valerie appeared in front of Mathew, her gloves and body coated with Cynthia's unique blood. "What now?"

"We level this place to the ground." Mathew stated as Lee landed in the middle of the group.

"Sorry, I got buried alive back there."

"Guys, we can't leave anything standing or alive." Mathew soberly said watching his friends with rubble debris and crater damage all around them.

"Diana, take everyone outside of the field. I'll take care of the rest." Lee said as his helmet became transparent, showing his head but still protecting it.

"Valerie." Mathew held out his hand. Valerie took his hand and both shrunk to the size of a fly, followed by Kyle and Cynthia. Diana waiting for them to enter her outside suit pocket.

"You okay?" Diana removed her goggles, revealing soft eyes surrounded by terrific makeup.

"I'm okay. This won't be the first time I kill people."

Diana held his hands in hers. "It won't be like this forever."

"I know. It's just hard trying to keep everyone alive." Lee's honesty was more than she really knew.

"Maybe you're trying too hard... Have a little bit of faith in us."

"Faith has never been the problem; it's those damn nukes that won't cooperate."

Diana kissed him. "Well, forget about them for now. I'll tell you what, show me what you can really do and I'll show you something new when we get home."

"You asked for it." Lee smiled as his helmet turned pitch black.

Diana phased her body and flew away towards the perimeter of the projected cloaking field.

Lee flew up as high as he could before passing the energy field. His helmet's optics reconfigured as he scanned for thermo and nuclear energy sources. The communication array was badly damaged which helped in filtering a mountain of wavelengths, thanks to Mathew and Valerie. Thermo signatures of humans beyond the array indicated they were in miniature self-contained chain of rooms. The accelerators and six nuclear power plants underneath the building like structures were easier to spot and identify from the new vantage point. Lee took his time in targeting all of the humans and what seemed to be critical energy junctions and support systems. Two laser canons came out of the top of his wrists and arms. His optics displayed a mesh of targets with depth, distance and composition of materials in between him and the targets. White flashes of light lit up the sky as Lee unleashed death upon every corner of the complex.

Pulsating laser beams split air, rock, metal, plastic and fresh with tremendous ease. Every structure caved downward with an unnatural lack of dust debris. Level upon level packed on top of each other as if all of the vertical beams and walls were shifted flat. Lee double-checked the area looking for any living beings. Once satisfied all humans were dead, he focused on the center nuclear reactor. He fired a tight constant beam at the reactor. The combination of his energy and nuclear material triggered an underground nuclear explosion. The ground shook as the seismic shockwave made its presence known. The outside air rushed in like a bizarre when the cloaking field disappeared only to be pushed back a little by the displacement of air near the ground. The earth at ground zero lifted up a hundred feet, then collapsed downward several hundred meters. The subterranean destruction extended way beyond where Diana waited in mid air.

Her awe was masked by silence as she hovered above the

devastated ground all around.

Lee flew with lightning speed stopping in front of her within arm's reach. "We need to leave. The Australians and other countries will quickly try to investigate what happened here."

"How did you do that?"

Lee hugged her and started flying back home as his armored suit wrapped around her. "I let gravity and physics do the work."

Chapter Ten

••◆••

I Like You More and More

Galloo Island, Henderson, New York

L ake Ontario glistened in the moonlight as fog started to creep onto the sandy shore. Stargazer stood inside a bunker two flights down. He slowly turned around scanning the grounds. To his dismay, the trees and plant life on the island limited his unique vision to extend up to the overgrown grass clinging to the bunker he occupied. He looked straight ahead seeing through the rock and intermittent roots, only to stop at the algae and plant life on the lake bed. He looked up seeing empty rooms and stars above, but it was little consolation since the androids would not be approaching from the sky.

"We're blind here." Stargazer faced one of two exit doors to the upper floors.

"Don't sweat it Star. Io and Creator can see them just as well as you can. Besides, all we have to do is attack anyone who's new to the island." Rat Bastard in rat form sat ready to fly up through the bunker and into the middle of battle.

"What if one of them impersonates Creator or me?"

Rat looked at Stargazer then at Spot, "Well it's a good thing I can't hurt you guys, but if I do, I apologize ahead of time."

"That's the spirit." Spot smiled as he sat on an empty supply crate.

Creator entered the fortified ammo storage area in an SIA armored suit with heavy-duty ballistics helmet. "Okay, you guys ready?" His SIA body armor and rifle looked authentic.

"Is that real?" Stargazer saw the moving parts and ammo in the assault rifle.

Creator stuck out the rifle in front of him looking at it for a second and then roughly put it next to Spot. "Of course it's real. What good would it do to have fake props?"

"We're ready." Rat Bastard stood on his hind legs.

"Hmm, okay. But you should be warned that if I were the enemy I would take out the fur ball with teeth before anyone else."

Rat Bastard stared him down with a low growl.

"He's joking with you." Stargazer readjusted a chest strap on his SIA issued dark colored camouflaged body armor.

"No, I'm not. Rats can hear you coming from mile away. First rule of combat is to take out any early warning systems. Come on; follow me." Creator said motioning Spot to pick up the rifle he left on the crate.

Rat Bastard smiled, turning back into his tall muscular self; wearing a two piece suit. "Someone finally appreciates my abilities."

The four men went upstairs and started their new assignment of walking the layered perimeters to give the impression of guarding the naval property. The old military training site had the needed facilities to house people on the run or in hiding. But it was far from being a fortification made to combat super machines.

Io and Ghost waited in a center room of the complex, with offices and classrooms taking up most of the area on the first floor. The first floor was not an ideal place for people to hide, but the intent was for the bait to be moderately accessible to the androids. Io looked exactly like Senator Warren; while Ghost sat next to him acting like a bodyguard would; playing on a laptop.

"So what happens if they attack one at a time to test our security?" Ghost looked at the one opened door into the room, with a long fold up table standing between the two men.

Io scanned the area seeing past a few walls until his thermo sensors couldn't penetrate them anymore. "They will send in a team of four while the rest secure a perimeter around the installation."

"Won't it be easier to send one guy and blow himself up to clear the building, then move in?" Ghost typed on the old laptop, playing solitaire.

"Humans have the idea that committing suicide under the guise of heroism or patriotism for a noble or ideological cause is a tactic which is effective. But as a Tantalumized being, I know they will not deploy that self defeating tactic. Worst case scenario, I would lobe a high explosive warhead strong enough to knockout all of the surface structures. Then I would move in with four androids to clear the center and have androids around the perimeter to provide suppressive fire and support."

"And least case scenario?"

"Five androids would enter through the five entryways mowing down anything in sight, with the rest shooting through all the exposed windows. Any superhumans which get in the way will be attacked directly with telepathic disrupters."

"What, why the hell didn't you mention this before?"

"I have analyzed everyone extensively and for some unknown reason, your group has a block against the telepathic disruptors which are made to paralyze the victim. Creator and EFL are also immune to this limited attack, which is why it is the least case scenario." Io said as he casually paid attention to Ghost's game play.

"Well since you put it that way, I should be expecting a mortar round of something to hit the roof."

"Yes, my dear boy. But I doubt it will be effective in determining which targets have been eliminated." Io spoke with Senator Warren's televised characteristics.

Ghost looked at him with interest. "You know that's a little freaky."

"I agree." Mirage's voice sounded right on top of them.

Ghost looked up at the fluorescent lights and paneling. "That's freaky too."

"You get used to it after a while." Mirage replied.

Io looked at Ghost more than trying to identify the location of Mirage's voice. Ghost stopped playing and folded his arms. "So how can you help in fighting these guys?"

"According to Io. Separating the head from the rest of the body does the trick and also keeps them from blowing up so easily."

Ghost half smirked with interest. "And you can do that?"

A composite aluminum plate appeared and flopped on top of the table causing the laptop to bounce up by a millimeter. Ghost lifted his head back in reflexive alarm. "Creator gave me twenty of those. I assume they're strong enough to keep the androids from reuniting their bodies."

Ghost picked up the heavy one inch thick plate. "You must be very strong?"

Io also looked at the plate with a touch. "This material will not be able to penetrate my exoskeleton."

"No, you're probably stronger than me and it doesn't have to penetrate anything. I will make it possible for it to be used as a weapon." Mirage's young sounding voice was masked by a veteran's confidence.

"Oh." Ghost's thoughts went to why he never considered using his phasing ability as a weapon.

The footsteps in the hallway drew their attention, as Creator came in; impersonating Vice President Donar. "How is everyone doing?"

"Who are you?" Ghost asked wondering if he were an android, but Io's inactivity eased his concern.

Creator looked at him. "I know you have skipped half a century of Fox news, but you don't know who the Vice President of the United

States is?

"The last I knew of Spiro Agnew was Vice President."

"Yeah, I remember him; especially after he resigned." Creator spoke with his own voice.

"He resigned?" Ghost's wonder was more from not being able to mentally read the three people in the room.

"Don't sweat it. You didn't miss much with politics, except for maybe when Quatris and Hellfire said they would not destroy a country because the American people didn't like them." Creator changed into a male SIA agent wearing standard low tactical coveralls. Resembling a police officer without the badge or utility belt, but had a shoulder hoister and handgun to match.

"Is that why they didn't stop South America from becoming one nation?" Ghost asked knowing a summary of the major events since his time traveling disappearance.

"I asked Quatris that question a long time ago." Creator looked through the buildings, scanning the area for androids as he spoke. "He said, the Colombian counsel had their reasons for enforcing their way of living on others. That is was a fight for humankind and if superhumans wanted to intervene, then they would have to go through him."

"I keep hearing that EFL is the most powerful superhuman group on the planet. How powerful is Quatris?"

Creator looked at Ghost in a relaxed standing posture. "Quatris or Hellfire could kill every living organism on the planet in minutes if they wanted to, but on the positive side, they won't and there are others who can fight back if need be."

"Why don't they go wipe out the androids?"

"Cuz, they're not on the planet. Plus, it's like taking a nuke to kill a cockroach in a city."

"Oh..." Ghost slowly closed the laptop in thought.

"Heads up people. Two androids to the east. Tell the rest." Creator commanded as he ran outside to get into position.

"Everyone, two androids to the east. Probably more all around." Ghost alerted the other three.

Standing on ground level, Stargazer looked around the island with intermittent patches of areas not blocked by vegetation. "I spot one two hundred meters north-northeast."

Ghost automatically relayed the information to Spot, Rat Bastard and Io. "Star says there is one two hundred meters north northeast."

"Erica, you got that?" Mirage said through her comlink, relaying the info to Creator and the others half a mile out."

"Yes." Erica's short talk was normal following practiced battle drill procedures.

Ghost stood up. "Io can handle the androids here. Maybe you should go keep Stargazer and Spot out of trouble."

"Where are they?" Mirage asked after a moment of thought.

"Spot's outside to the left of the door. Star's on the opposite side."

"Swell." Her voice trailed by the door.

"What's wrong?" Io asked looking at Ghost.

"I still don't know how I can help. I can't do anything to hurt any android."

"You can be a distraction while I take them out from behind." Io suggested thinking of his exact strategy.

Ghost pursed his lips a little as he smiled. "I like that."

Spot walked slowly along the northern wall of the outermost building. The shifting of air pressure raised too rapidly as an android occupied the space behind him. Spots enhanced senses and reactive instincts kicked in. He swung around with a lightning fast leg sweep. The impact and superhuman strength of his leg would have split through a bank's vault door but instead only toppled the android on his side. The android's right leg as deformed into a near right angle as Spot stuck out his hand in front of the android's face.

The android's head didn't bend or bounce off the ground as his shoulder imbedded itself into the partially grass covered ground. A laser beam from Spot's hand burned into his head with the grass around the area catching fire. Cinders of grass and smothering earth ten meters behind the android made a visible mark as the head was almost instantly liquefied. The setting sun cast a shadow over the now burning wall along the building. Spot sprang up on his feet expecting the android to explode having blasted him with full power with his intense innate laser ability.

'Huh, Io said they wouldn't explode if the head damage was quick and extensive' Spot thought but the inactivity of the neutralized android distracted him.

A pair of hands reached out from behind him and another pair to his front. The teleportation of the androids was sensed especially with the visual of the android facing him. Spot punched and raised his other arm deflecting the frontal attack. His fist made solid contact, but only bounced off the android's nose with an ear screeching metallic clang.

With a quick step forward, Spot tried to swing downward with his extended hand used to deflect the android's grabbing attempt, and force the android to the ground. With uncanny balance the android stepped backward over Spot's foot, while two hands grabbed Spot's shoulders from behind. A stabbing kick pounced on the back of Spot's knee as he was pushed down and backwards from his shoulders.

Spot strained to fly out of their grasp, only to carry the two androids a few feet along the ground. The android to his front hugged Spot, body slamming him and the other android into the ground. The androids manhandled Spot forcing his face into the dirt.

Spot screamed as excruciating pain ripped through his right arm. Pinned in the prone both androids had the clear advantage as Spot's right arm bent upwards; his hand and forearm folding onto his back as the arm broke at the elbow.

Spot twisted his head to get a glimpse of the two assailants. He yelled again, but in anger as he couldn't push or twirl out of his painful and deadly predicament. He saw the android's head get large to his right come at his face barely scraping his cheek as the head rolled away. The wet dirt and grassy smell mixed in with a new metallic aroma. The heavy weight on his back eased as the other android's head also bounced and rolled inches from his face. He used his good arm to get on three limbs. Two metallic disks Mirage had shown Ghost earlier hit the ground in unison as the android's bodies flopped to the ground on both sides.

"Don't move, I'm going to reconnect your forearm back into

position." Mirage's voice was right next to Spot's ear sounding over the painful thoughts of what she was about to do. In the distance an explosion rumbled the ground for a brief second.

Spot looked down at his arm as the forearm dangled touching the few blades of flatten grass. The pain almost instantly vanished as the forearm turned a dark phantom like texture. Mirage's feminine figure in the same phantom appearance was knelt next to him holding his forearm and hand with both of hers. She carried a backpack and he could make out a camouflage outline on her clothes, skin and hair distinguished by various colors. He was sure the colors would be brilliant and contrasting if the dark phantom texture was not present, making them all different shades of tinted gray. She twisted the forearm into the right position.

"What the hell?" Spot whispered as she moved her fingers into his phased forearm and elbow; repositioning the bone connections, ligaments, veins and muscle.

"Okay, stand up." Mirage stood with him as she let go of him.

Without mercy, the pain returned as he clucked his elbow with his left hand, not needing to since his superhuman makeup made his arm like steel, even in a broken state. He composed himself, releasing the elbow, but making sure not to bend it, knowing the pain would increase.

"I'm down guys." He said and thought, hoping Ghost was tracking the battle, hearing fighting within and outside of the complex, even though his regenerated arm would be well in a few minutes. He turned towards the center of the complex only to see an android teleport in front of him.

Mirage disappeared and in a fraction of a second so did Spot. The android looked intently scanning his front, but as he turned his head for a wider scan, a metallic disk appeared in his neck. The body of the android entered Mirage's and Spot's world for a fraction of a second as the disk and head fell to the ground. Spot was amazed as Mirage held his hand and with her other hand controlled the molecular structure of the android's headless body.

Spot could see Mirage clearly now as he too was phased and invisible with her. It was unlike his experience with Ghost. The specter and white aspect of his past experience was replaced with almost perfect color and solid appearance as if they were HD holograms which no one could see. Mirage was very young with short fluffy hair each strand a different hue out of over thousands of combinations. Her face was masked camo designs, with her eyes of various greens and yellows. She was a few inches shorter than him and her slender stature was simple with no clearly defined muscles. It made her very attractive in many respects as she had smooth curves from head to toe.

She turned to him maintaining a tight hold of his left hand. "Stay with me so I won't have to save you again."

Spot smiled in awe by the ease of her deadly efficiency.

Stargazer walked down a hallway as the sneak attack on Spot forced the androids' hand. He peered through the wood and plaster walls monitoring a female android teleport just inside the main building. Without delay, Stargazer flew through two walls dead center into the android's gut. The two burst through the cinderblock of the outer wall and bounced several times along a clearing and between trees. A wrecking ball paled in comparison to the instant demolition of the reinforced wall. The slender physic of the android was very deceiving as she held an iron grip around Stargazer's back.

The two came to a complete stop at the base of an oak tree. Stargazer felt her release one hand and place it on the back of his head. He twirled around counterclockwise forcing her upper body into the ground. She left up her touch on his head as he flew up as fast as he could through tree branches above the trees and back down into the ground. The rustling of leaves and breaking of branches followed by a resounding thump of earth shaking the ground as Stargazer embraced the android's explosive heat and energy turning up a large ten foot crater.

Io and Ghost stood at the ready inside their assigned room. Spot's early warning wasn't enough to prepare them as six androids male and female teleported inside the room. Io teleported almost instantly behind one, grabbing his head and twisting it off with a snapping metallic sound. Ghost vanished as two androids with miniguns shot at where he and Io used to be. The androids were expertly placed as the armor piercing bullets tunneled an area between them on the opposite side of the room. The fire was short as they realized Io was already attacking a second android and what they thought was a SIA agent was gone.

In a matter of seconds, the androids analyzed their situation and converged on Io. "Teleport away, I'll take care of them!" Ghost yelled into Io's mechanical consciousness.

Five androids surrounded Io as he teleported outside fifty feet straight up. Ghost concentrated and quickly sent a transmutation command into the four functional androids in the room.

He flew through the wall into the hallway and transmuted two other androids in the passages as four explosions pushed the inners of the building in all directions. Splintered wood, metal and plaster debris scattered everywhere as two other explosions added to the acceleration of damage.

Creator walked out on the south side as an android teleported behind him and karate chopped his neck. The deadly hand would have sliced a normal human's head clean off, but Creator's neck absorbed most of the physical attack's energy while his essence simply resisted the Tantalumized hardness. Creator swung around with extreme speed, uncanny even for most superhumans. His left palm instantly found the back of the android's neck, while he leaped and placed his right palm on the assassin's face. A telekinetic energy blot erupted out of his right palm. The android's head seemed to rip away from the body as if it were made of liquid melting from a high pressured blowtorch.

The telekinetic blot took the shredded head and created a trench ten meters long and two meters deep at the end point. The android's body fell to the ground as Creator turned into the appearance of the android that just tried to kill him. He looked out into the wood line seeing nothing, but when his scan went to the other side of the island near the mainland of New York, he spotted twelve androids. Eight of them teleported into the building and room Io and Ghost occupied. He flew up above the roof hoping to get a clear line of sight on the four androids by the perimeter. The explosions below him didn't sway his plan as he darted straight at the left flank android. The androids turned their attention to Creator as he stopped next to the left side android. A large telekinetic blot came out of Creator's fists splitting the immediate assassin in half, tearing through everything in its path. Trees and two other androids encountered a piercing shift of matter in two cubic feet of destruction extending out to the water several hundred meters beyond.

The androids exploded like a daisy chain countering the building debris now failing to rain on trees extending to the shore. The android he missed teleported out of sight, so he scanned around for other signs of activity looking through debris standing structure and underground compartments. "Starfire how's it going up there?" Creator spoke as his comlink moved out of his wrist into the open while he transformed into his superhero outfit.

"Four are neutralized." Starfire's voice was calm as the southern sky lit up red and then white, for a few seconds as if a small meteor made impact ten miles away.

Creator flew up above the rubble and smothering fires. Rat Bastard forced himself out of a pile of roofing, stood up in his two piece suit and stylishly dusted his arm clean mimicking a secret agent cliché.

"Stargazer and Spot please come to me" Creator instructed through his comlink as he flew down to Rat Bastard's location.

Io was first to come to their side with Spot and Mirage appearing second. Ghost flew up to them as Stargazer flew swiftly from the east, his back all covered in dirt while his upper clothing and SIA body armor was blown off down to his skin. "This reminds me of a trend." Spot joked as he started to slowly bend his elbow.

"I need you guys to scan the area for any androids we missed." Creator said.

"We need to destroy the remaining bodies." Io warned.

Everyone except Ghost looked at him. "Why?" Several of them said in unison.

"Unlike most technology, a person could take the heads and reconnect them to the bodies. It is theoretically conceivable the android can be brought back to life outside of the confines of their original laboratory."

"The androids are like zombies." Rat Bastard smiled.

"I can't find anything android-ish like." Stargazer said trying to motivate the others to scan as Creator instructed.

After a moment, Creator spoke through his comlink. "You guys have anything?"

"Negative Boss." Night replied.

"Okay come to our location and bring all the scraps with you."

It wasn't long before three flying objects came to their location from three different vectors. It was clear there were no android remains due to Starfire's and Starlight's intense area-effect energy which disintegrated the Tantalumized particles into liquid vapor.

Stargazer's group stared at Starfire and Starlight's elegant and mesmerizing landings. Starfire's red flames and Starlight's glowing yellowish white light aura made a definite statement as two members of Energy Fire and Light (EFL).

"Five Ghosts, this is Starfire and Starlight, as you already know Night." Creator introduced the two women.

"Your wives of Quatris and Hellfire." Ghost stated before any hellos could be made, seeing that Rat Bastard was about to ask one of them out.

"Yes, we are. It's quite an honor to meet people from the past." Starfire said as her flames fizzled out when she shook their hands.

"Nice to meet you." Starlight's glowing blond hair was as comely as her friend's goddess like appearance.

"Before we collect the android pieces for disposal, what's the plan? I counted twenty-one androids. Which is a lot more than what was expected" Creator turned to face Io and Stargazer.

"Well now we." Stargazer pointed at his group and Io. "Need to contact South America and see if they will help us take out the mountain complex in Australia where the androids are being manufactured and trained."

"You didn't mention that in your earlier plan?" Creator calmly said.

"No, it was a plan in progress. Now that you have seen and changed the game, we can go destroy the plant, while you guys seek and destroy the androids on the loose. Chances are that once the plant is destroyed, they will be ordered back home for defense."

"Erica, tell Max we will clean the area, so not to move in with his clean-up team. I will call him later about what to do with the targets." Creator said without raising his comlink to his mouth.

"I can help you get in touch with South America." Starfire stated, everyone even Starlight looked in her direction.

"Good, because we don't want to start a national incident or war pointing at the U.S. government or you guys. But if it were me, they would just have exaggerated headlines about my good looks and Rat's long tail." Stargazer joked.

Creator smiled. "I like you more and more."

"Why is that?"

"I thought I was the only one who gave Max gray hairs. Now I know someone had some sympathy on him by sending you away for half a century."

Ghost almost laughed as he mentally saw Spot and Rat Bastards' convoluted agreement with the comment.

Chapter Eleven

Good Hunting

Twenty Thousand feet above Bogota, Colombia

S tarfire led the group in flight; all holding hands and quite visible as Ghost couldn't cloak Io's molecular structure. The expected air defense system was open to approach ever since they entered South American airspace many miles to the north. No escort or threatening planes or missiles plagued them. Stargazer suspected there was some kind of agreement between EFL and the super power. It gave him great comfort to know these powerful superhumans trusted the nation controlled by a five member council, many times referred to by opposing media the council of dictators; the four horsemen plus one by Mideast countries. Comfort to know Quatris was probably the one superhuman Cyer rivaled. Comfort to know Quatris wasn't alone, and if South America was a force working for good, then they had a chance without destroying the planet in the process.

Ghost and Rat Bastard enjoyed the hypersonic scenery even

though the landings were scary to witness; as if they were about to plow into the ground or city block, but instead came to an almost complete stop without the fatal gravitational hazards. Their unusual landing on a street clearing by the side of a mountain caused for some questions. "Wow, are we here for a pit stop?" Rat Bastard asked seeing a corner store and several rows of geodesic homes parallel to the street winding around the mountain. All the structures proudly displaying solar panels, fiberglass alloyed framing, highly resistant privacy windows and eco friendly landscaping.

Starfire smiled. "You remind me of Scott when he was younger."

"Really, wow." Rat Bastard's eyes widen as his appetite was compared to Quatris.

Stargazer looked at the intermittent holes of earth he could penetrate with his vision. "I think they got better food underground."

Starfire glanced at him. "You can see the underground fortress?"

"Yes." Stargazer canted his head. "Am I not supposed to?"

"Guard what you know. If it fell in the wrong hands, people could die needlessly." She casually walked to the side of the street as a few electrically powered cars passed by.

Spot watched the pedestrians and occupants of the dwellings, mostly elderly and children in their homes, performing office work or playing games. The quality and high tech level of living was drastic compared to the rest of the world, which reminded him of the Arlos society in Andromeda, minus the flying cars.

The overcast of sparse clouds helped in showcasing the marvelous designs and light reflections of glass and colors of Bogota's skyscrapers and very organized layout. "Why aren't we down there talking to the council members?" Stargazer asked, staying by Starfire's side.

"The Ramerize brothers rarely have time to spend in the city, traveling all over the continent. It is also rare that one will see you. This is where I was told he would meet us." Starfire's superhero costume instantly changed to an elegant white dress decoratively trimmed with black and red lines.

The rest of the group wore dress suits, making them stick out as if there was a convention of lost businessmen.

A sleek white and silver shuttle rolled to a stop next to them as if an invisible bus stop sign was posted. The entire top had solar panels and the tinted windows deceptively ensured privacy. The street was very wide with four lanes and the bus made very good use of space; holding twelve men all in complete body armor. Stargazer looked at every detail of weaponry. He could swear they all had a side arm and a light saber looking weapon. As Starfire started to board with the sliding door fully open, he determined the saber handles were extendable antenna like foils with an end cap.

The shuttle itself was heavily armored with a two inch thick type of fiberglass alloy; similar to the makeup of the body armor on all of the men. Starfire led the way as six seats were conveniently left open in the center of the bus facing the center.

"Nice, this is like a subway car." Rat Bastard said as he looked at the men all wearing their helmets, half with rifles at the ready in front of their chest plates.

The driver closed the door once all were onboard and sped off down the road. Starfire pointed at the seats making sure Stargazer sat between her and one of the Soldiers.

Stargazer saw the men's faces through their flat black helmets recognizing Edward Ramerize. "Mr. Ramerize." He extended a hand.

"Welcome Stargazer. I've heard a lot about you." Eduardo spoke in perfect English.

"Really?" Stargazer doubted, hoping Ghost would fill him in.

'I can't read any of them.' Ghost mentally answered him.

"Don't be alarmed. I have to have telepaths with me at all times for security purposes. I know why you came, but it's a very complicated thing you're asking for. But excuse my manners, Welcome all of you. It's been a while since you visited." Eduardo's visor turned transparent as he smiled at Starfire.

"It's been almost two decades." Starfire's smile was mutual.

"I hope next time it will be for a vacation, you and Scott would love our beaches and mountain retreats."

"I'll make sure we do."

Spot and Stargazer noticed the guards around Io being very attentive to his actions, ready to react at any sign of danger. "Excuse me, but you don't need to fear Io." Ghost stated.

"Normally I would agree with you, but we have been visited by your type in the past. It's only a precaution since we don't know you well enough. Starfire is here to ensure nothing happens. No insult intended." Eduardo turned his head toward Io.

"None taken." Io casually replied continually analyzing everything in sight, like a tourist on a scientific adventure.

Eduardo smirked at his sincerity. "We're familiar with the mountain complex in Australia, but we don't have enough specifics to be able to perform a surgical assault on it. We weren't even sure if it was the only place the androids were created, until now. Since time is a factor, I am willing to send you in with a team. If you can't complete the mission, we will have to go with a backup plan by using overt force."

"There are many people who fear a third world war, why are you so accommodating?" Stargazers asked what Spot and Ghost wanted to know.

Eduardo looked at the men's faces as if trying to choice a winner of some competition. "My brother told me to trust you. Younger siblings tend to be more trusting of people, but there's one thing I learned during the wars I fought as a grunt and as a leader." He removed his helmet. An act his bodyguards clearly disliked, many placing their hands on their sabers or handguns ready for a quick draw.

Eduardo's black hair was cut short as expected for professional Soldiers, his brown eyes were clear without bags under them to show any fatigue as his smile proved his ability to inspire joy from the people experiencing his presence. "Wars aren't won by a single person, they're won with many people that are bond together as a family with hopefully a noble cause."

Stargazer was silent but he slowly nodded in agreement. The others were silent as well looking at the Soldiers as the bus eased into a stop.

"What Estabon and I started decades ago wasn't to grain power or fame. We created this federation and powerful nation to help people. War unfortunately has been one of those methods. I must attend to my duties now. I wish you well and good hunting." Eduardo put his helmet back on and walked outside followed by the elite squad of bodyguards.

The shuttle had stopped in front of a bunker entrance. Tables and chairs were setup with an eatery style decor outside; almost completely camouflaging the personnel entrance into an underground complex at ground level. Many people in warm almost new clothes blended with several hundred Soldiers in body armor, almost all carrying their helmets attached to their sides; except for Eduardo's escort.

Stargazer led the group out with Starfire last. Most eyes turned towards Eduardo as he mingled with the crowd, but many still looked at the men and Starfire. Ghost sensed indications of various reasons for the stares, many honoring Eduardo as a Councilmember his five silver diamond insignia on his collar and escort hailing his presence, all Soldiers and even some civilians it seemed saluted the man and his escort. Others wanted to see the beautiful redhead and the men that rode with the Councilman.

A tall middle aged Soldier stood in Stargazer's path, without a helmet in sight. "Sir, I have been instructed to give your team a good lunch experience before you go meet with one of our ships in the Southern Ocean." He said in almost perfect English, with a hint of a French accent.

"What's on the menu?" Stargazer glanced back at Rat Bastard.

"We have an assortment of meats, soups, pastries, ice creams and natural fruit drinks."

The Soldier extended his hand to the side like a waiter pointing them to a reserved table under a large awning.

"Do we have time to eat?" Stargazer grinned waiting for an

immediate reply.

"We have enough time." Rat Bastard walked ahead smelling the sweet aromas of the roasting steak, chicken and trout mingled with arepas and chorizo.

As the group sat, Eduardo and his escort were already entering the bunker entrance, gracefully leaving the area.

The meals were cooked to perfection and with speed. Everyone had a great time speaking to Soldiers and civilians seated in adjacent tables. The rumors of evil things from their history and reputation seemed to vanish as they saw the people speak positively about themselves and other countries. Starfire was impressed by the six star service along the country side and the advancements they had made in less than thirty years. She sort of kicked herself for not visiting earlier when Quatris and Hellfire came to the continent on business. "You know I will take up that offer on a vacation." She whispered to herself.

Rat Bastard started to speak, "Star...." "Rebecca, if I may call you that?" Ghost interrupted.

Starfire turned to Ghost who was sitting across from her and Rat Bastard. "Yes, it's quite alright, ever since we went public, I like being called by my birth name."

"Rat Bastard was wondering if you know of some eligible female he could meet and perhaps also take on a vacation."

Rebecca laughed. "This has to be the first time anyone has asked me to be a matchmaker."

"Why are you encouraging him?" Stargazer looked at Ghost.

'Because he was about to ask her if he could hook up with her sister or cousin.' Ghost mentally and privately replied.

"Oh." Stargazer sternly glared at Rat Bastards almost pathetic facial expression of a mouthful of food and half smile. "You don't have to Rebecca. Rat Bastard likes to hit on any woman he thinks will pay attention to him."

"It's okay, I know a lot of single girls. But we'll have to wait until all of this assassination stuff is over with." Her carefree attitude and openness was disarming, considering she used to be very prominent hardnosed lawyer before EFL went public.

"Yes, you are correct. So now that it looks like we're all done. How do we get to the ship you were talking about?" Ghost asked the guide.

"Mr. Ghost, I was informed your group could fly to the Southern Ocean. Here is a coordinate for the linkup." The Soldier extended a large digital wristwatch above the table, a GPS readout indicated the longitude and latitude plus several countdown times. "Once at the location, the ship will contact you through the band."

"Master would have liked this trip." Spot said as Ghost passed the wristband to Stargazer.

"If all goes well, everyone will get a chance to relax and enjoy the good things in life once again." Stargazer stood up. "Io. I will take you. The three of you stay invisible and close. Rebecca, I think it will be best if we parted ways here. Once the mission is completed, we will head back to link up with Creator. Hopefully Master will have come up with a plan on what's next."

The group moved away from the UV fabric shading. In a fraction of a second, Rebecca's dress transformed into her Starfire costume. Io turned into a very large backpack. Stargazer smiled not having to hold his hand halfway around the world. He flew off with Io, while the other three disappeared under Ghost's power; Spot taking off after their leader. Starfire waited a moment looking at Stargazer hit Mach 5. "Good luck guys." She flew off to the north.

The audience in the neighborhood and mountainside looked on in wonder. Not that they had never seen superhumans in action, but more of what it implied with Starfire being one of those in their midst for a brief moment as it was.

Thirty minutes into the flight the group mentally communicated going over the mountain defenses. But there was a gaping hole in their strategy because it would be hard to get Io close to the mountain without attracting attention. "Do you find it kind of easy that the complex is near the water?" Spot stated what everyone for some reason seemed never to consider.

"The vicinity of the mountain to the water facilitates easy access for the androids to be transported to other locations with greater secrecy. The energy needed to sustain the demands of the manufacturing process would require several nuclear sources. The planetary sensors regulating nuclear material and weapons were placed before we developed the ability to cloak it. Geothermal and wave energy became the solution in being able to power the complex without attracting attention. The mining activity next to the mountain also allows for a plausible cover to move a lot of personnel and equipment in and out of the area." Io explained with a hint of pride for the accomplishment.

"So you guys can cloak a nuclear power plant?" Stargazer's interest was sparked.

"Yes, but the technology is recent which has been used sparingly."

"What else does it cloak?" Stargazer watched the GPS location changing its coordinates every few minute increments.

"If cloaks any group output of energy spectrums."

"Could it hide a city or ship?"

"It is possible, but I don't think we have developed it to such a large-scale or small enough for it to be portable."

Stargazer looked out into the ocean. The moving target on the water wasn't there and he couldn't penetrate the chloroform particles underneath. Sonic booms rang across the waters, several commercial and two military vessels could only speculate to the source far beyond the range of their electronic sensors. Stargazer hovered above the seawater looking towards the west and pushed the arrival icon on the wristband.

"Are we here?" Rat Bastard asked his voice coming out of thin air.

"That's what the GPS says." Stargazer held up the wristband.

Io transformed off of Stargazer's back into his normal human figure but kept a hand on Star's shoulder so he wouldn't plummet into the ocean.

"It's moving" Spot stared at the digital readout.

Stargazer looked into the water, his vision penetrated fifty feet before the density of plankton turned everything black. Spot however noticed a shadow approaching them as if a whale or submarine had found them.

The dark outline of a massive ship rippled out of the water cutting through the waves. Elevated smooth turrets and a center structure replaced the normal ship's weather deck. Stargazer had difficulty seeing deep into the ship, but it was clear the turrets held missiles, shells and a laser like weapon. The center structure held the setup of an aircraft carrier for command and control. As the ship approached the two men, it slowed drastically countering the flowing motion of water. A hatch slide open, revealing a landing platform for a helicopter or vertical takeoff plane. There were no outside markings or evident creases, but Stargazer saw twelve platforms; six in the bow and six in the stern.

The three heroes appeared in the visible light spectrum alongside of Stargazer and Io. "That's some ship?" Spot said knowing the many issues and practical use of making a submergible ship.

The group flew down into the bay; several rotary and fixed winged aircrafts seemed to be positioned ready for a quick launch on short notice off to the side. Stargazer could see better once inside the ship, not having to compete with the outside plant life. Everything seemed to have been constructed with the same or various modifications of the fiberglass and metallic alloy used on armor for the Soldiers and homes in Bogota. "They're using some specialized woven glass and metal alloy on all of the bracing and support materials, this is keeping them from taking up massive amounts of space like a battleship... everything is made of this stuff." Stargazer stated as he knelt and touched the platform, the outer layered doors sliding shut, a soft alarm indicating a tight seal.

A squad of Soldiers walked up on the platform led by a man dressed in a padded suit more conducive for swimming should he be left out at sea. "Welcome aboard, Five Ghosts." The man spoke with a southern Alabama accent.

"How is everyone all of the sudden calling us as the Five Ghosts?" Spot whispered.

"They must have got your email." Stargazer stood up and faced the reception party. "Thank you, I'm Stargazer."

"I didn't know you had an email account?" Rat Bastard looked at Spot.

"I don't." Spot turned a frown at Rat then smiled. "Master must have done something."

'Or maybe they read all of our minds when we talked to Eduardo.' Ghost mentally said as Lt. Commander Jimenez introduced himself.

'I feel so violated.' Rat Bastard thought as Stargazer introduced the entire group.

'That won't be the first time.' Spot smiled thinking of the time Rat was caked with worm guts.

The group was quickly escorted to a large rehearsal and operational battle room. As they walked towards the room the ship dove back into the vastness of arctic tempered waters.

Unlike the spaceships and space station in the Andromeda galaxy, the group was not allowed to roam or venture out more than necessary. Food was brought to them and they had access to a bed in an open bay connected to the battle room. Five alpha and beta teams were present for the briefing on their plan of attack on the complex. The ship would be in position seven hours from their linkup. It was very impressive since the ship had to travel five hundred miles undetected by other submarines or sonar screens. Rehearsals were conducted along with contingencies; should they be compromised at any point of the operation.

Stargazer was concerned about the amount of Soldiers involved. A beta team consisted of twenty five Soldiers and the alpha teams had nine Soldiers each. The rehearsals paid dividends, demonstrating the expertise of the elite professionals. The two beta teams were for security and support just outside of the objective, while the three alpha teams were to go with the heroes into the mountain.

Ghost was highly impressed by the knowledge of everyone. The alpha team members all knew seven languages fluently and a dozen more conversationally. All were sniper trained and cross trained with all of the American Special Forces disciplines. They were all also very hard to read. Spot surmised all of the South American citizens had to some degree been mentally enhanced or trained, allowing them to have so many skills and tons of scholarly knowledge.

Stargazer analyzed the five lieutenants, each understanding very well what was at stake, as if the Captain or someone higher up the chain of command gave them full disclosure and authority for what needed to be done. The Captain himself visited for an hour inspecting the troops, but mostly watched the newcomers to make sure his ship wasn't in danger. Stargazer ensured the teams knew the weaknesses the androids possessed. Io once again ran down all of the vulnerable spots and standard battle drills, which constituted major damage and clear disregard for human life.

"Whatever you do, the most important thing you can do when in front of an android no matter if it looks like an injured old woman is to inflict as much damage as you can at the center of the neck. Do not hesitate." Io's stern and serious stare dug deep into all of the men and women's eyes.

"And a karate chop or single bullet will never do it." Io continued.

"Mr. Io. We understand how much force is necessary. And we will use it. If all goes to plan, we won't have to get into a free for all." The ranking leader, Lieutenant Chin, calmly stated.

Io turned his head to Stargazer. Star's nod gave an indication to continue. Stargazer watched the weaponry on the mission, all high powered munitions with explosive warheads. Each Soldier carried two sabers and many different types of grenades. If they did get into a free for all, it would be a messy one and he was betting the androids might have met their match.

The seventh hour came and eighty-one humans and one android left the ship underwater. The submersibles silently took the attack force swiftly through the water. The Soldiers didn't use scuba gear and relied on the armored suits to maintain an internal environment. The crafts were shaped like dolphins, the flippers use to drag a chain of Soldiers behind them. The group except for Io was given water suits similar to all the operators in the ship.

As the teams came within waist deep water among the waves, the crafts were released. Without delay, the unmanned crafts sped off on a return trip to the ship, leaving the Soldiers committed to the mission.

Not a word was said among the Soldiers, or at least none that was heard outside of their helmets. The beach was rocky with trees embracing the high tide waters. The ear pieces provided to the group helped greatly to hear the teams maneuver with exceptional precision to locations and security markers.

"It's time Ghost and I go on ahead. We will let you know if there are any issues." Stargazer said.

"Understood, but remember that our communications will not work once you turn invisible." Chin replied.

"Yeah we know. See you in five miles." Stargazer said and disappeared from sight.

The company size element melted into the dense vegetation as easily as the inhabitant wildlife. The eight and a half kilometers of jungle and sparse openings experienced light footsteps along with high tech environment generators. Each Soldier transmitted a normal early night's vibrations from sounds and rodent movement. The wildlife they disturbed were masked by the electronic emitters, hitting the ground surveillance radars as they approached the mountain side.

Stargazer and Ghost flew above the trees, covering the stretch within minutes. 'These guys and gals are scary serious.' Ghost said as he saw what Stargazer saw on the way to the beach.

'Yeah, their suits blend in with the surrounding thermo signatures, it's not perfect but you have to get up close to see the difference. They probably have something for other detection systems.' Stargazer hovered above an entry way guarded by Regular Australian Soldiers. But they knew better. The Soldiers didn't have to be androids; they were there to act as a tripwire. There were many ways to detect if any of the living warm bodies died or were incapacitated.

Stargazer scanned their clothing and bodies with great detail. 'There.' He stated as if he could point to it. 'They're wearing body monitors. If one of them coughs, whoever's on the other end will know about it.'

'So we go with plan B?' Ghost said as he looked out to the northwest.

'Yeah. Okay let's get somewhere safe and I will inform them.' Stargazer flew to the northwest into the jungle.

Ghost let go of Stargazer as he floated midair deep inside a tree. "This is Ghost 1. Security personnel have body monitors, need to change to plan Bravo. We're at ORP Bravo now."

"Roger, on our way." Chin's impressed voice was static free.

Stargazer vanished once again as the two men kept a look out for the teams and possible enemies.

The cloud cover made the jungle almost pitch black if it is wasn't for the super moon's chaw on the upper layers. The Soldiers saw an environment full of bright colors and clear land features, as if they could also see through matter like Stargazer.

Two hours passed as three teams entered the objective rally point along with the three other ghosts. Twenty-four men and three women spread out into three cigar formations, creating a wedge. There was no movement of Soldiers to the center or any movement around getting a headcount. All coordination and logistics was conducted through their secure internal comms. After a while Stargazer and Spot concluded the Soldiers were being managed individually on certain aspects by a command center, possibly the ship.

'There's no way they're talking to each other without sending out radio signals whether they're secure or not.' Stargazer mentally commented, seeing Io as the one obvious target according to what the Australians or androids could detect. But somehow he was being masked by the presence of the Soldiers.

'I think they're communicating directly to a satellite with laser communications.' Rat Bastard replied.

'What? How did you make that connection?' Ghost's surprised reply was felt.

'Laser communication back in Arlos was more advanced, but that's how Lix was able to get a hold of her men to find us. Maybe that is why they have no problem talking in the clear, because someone would have to be in the middle of the laser beam, be able to detect it and then know how to decipher it. And I thought you guys were smarter. Oh, have you guys been thinking about this all this time?' Rat Bastard's smile and confusion was felt.

'Good job big guy.' Stargazer smiled as he whispered into his mic piece. "Okay, Lieutenant Chin, whenever you guys are ready, we will take nine of you at a time."

"Our last beta team will be in position in thirty seconds."

"Roger. We'll wait."

Ghost prepared himself as he relaxed and moved to the center of the first alpha team.

Stargazer moved next to Io. "So you think you came get in there undetected?"

"Yes, but depending on the data cycle, we won't know how many Adams and Eves will be inside regeneration modules, until we get inside pass the simulators."

Stargazer thought and watched Ghost made an Alpha team and Spot disappear into a different fold of existence. "I should have asked

Mirage if she could make you disappear."

Io looked at him, then out into the darkness. "You humans are very slow to come up with solutions."

"Yeah, well you didn't think of it any faster." Stargazer whispered and positioned himself with the second team.

Ghost entered the complex high on the mountain side using the vent filtration system as a guide. They easily moved through the rock and manmade structures into a storage room and corner of a chemical refinement room. The team in the mountain went black from the outside, but kept internal comms, as Ghost quickly returned to pickup Stargazer and team two.

Team two appeared as a unit on the twentieth level of the sixty-four level complex. Stargazer could see the vast complex housing hundreds of android chambers and many sections with metallurgy machinery. "Tell Io the location is clear." Stargazer told Ghost before he left to get team three and Rat Bastard.

A minute later, Io teleported into empty laboratory Stargazer and team two occupied. The vibrations of air around Io faded away as he looked up and around the large room. "They know we're here."

Stargazer thought in alarm and looked at Io's focused direction. Cameras were emplaced within the ceiling panels, unseen to the naked eye except for the neon lights. "They're new." 'Ghost return and get the teams out.'

"Why haven't they reacted?" Chin asked standing next to Stargazer pointing his assault weapon at one of two entrance doors.

"They're waiting to see if more people all of the sudden appear out of nowhere. But I have a feeling they will if they see one of the teams disappear." Stargazer replied.

"Okay, we go with last resort." Chin turned pointing in all directions. The team spread out around the room with the Soldiers in the center crouching low, all placing a hand on a saber with a rifle aimed slightly up with the other hand.

'Ghost, warn the others so they can start exfiltration. Once all of the people are outside, let me know so I can get out of the mountain.' Stargazer thought and looked at Io. "Once the shit hits the fan you protect the Soldiers, I will divert everything to me. Once Ghost gets these guys out, you teleport out to them and continue protecting them."

Stargazer stood at the center of the room, waiting for good news. He saw through the helmet visors, seeing brave anticipation of a fire fight in the making. Problem was they weren't used to exploding assassins. He scanned up and down seeing major movement closer to ground level. Androids were being assembled along with humans. Support personnel were being moved away from entry ways and hallways. A large number of androids assumed the appearance of technicians and security operators as if nothing was wrong. 'Do you see this?'

'Yes, I'll show the guys' Ghost instantly replied; grabbing a hold of the chain of Soldiers along with Spot, transporting them out of their assigned locations.

Stargazer braced his right foot back and shot his body out of the lab through the insulated sheet metal walls into the main center where Dr. Lethorn Harlov's desk resided. No humans were in sight; but three hundred androids stood in front of their training modules turning their heads in unison at Stargazer flying like a torpedo twenty feet above them in the several hundred meter long rectangular room.

Chapter Twelve

◆◆◆◆◆

These Guys Are Different

Malleson Corp, New York City

Tapping on the glass counter by healthy long glossy clear nails increased in rhythm as the Malleson elevator doors opened. The beautiful receptionist jumped up with excitement almost plowing her chair into the back counter wall. Three unarmed men in SWAT like uniforms quickly walked towards her. She likewise stepped around the desk to the side and opened Mathew's double door holding it for the men to pass.

Mathew and Valerie waited patiently in front of his ten foot wide charcoal oak table. Two of the men stopped just inside the office, while the leader continued withdrawing a data stick from his chest pocket. "What did you find Alex?" Valerie skipped all introductory pleasantries.

"Ma'am. If I may?" He held the data stick as he faced her, but she stepped aside and let him walk around to place the information in Mathew's computer.

The three moved behind the computer, Mathew allowed the investigator to sit on his linen chair.

Alex quickly opened a video and digital geographic report. One of two monitors on the table went full scale with a remote desert scene of a base similar to the one Lee destroyed, but with less above ground structures. The long range camera spotted two robotic androids. It was uncertain if there were men underneath the dull white helmet and armored body parts. Even when the robots ran at the camera faster than a speeding car; it was plausible for a man to be enhanced by the armored suit. But the teleportation and a zoom in on the weapon attached to their arms confirmed there was no human inside the attackers. The camera view moved chaotically in all directs as the investigator ran away. Sound of the metallic contact on the hard sand and bangs from the bullets tearing into the investigative team turned the male screams into a silent death.

The view went black and Alex placed the geographic report on full screen. "The team was able to transmit it live. Once we got it in the center, we flew here to get it to you. The location of the encounter is here." Alex pointed to a zoomed in map of Africa.

"Niger." Valerie said as she controlled the zooming of the area seeing nothing but desert; but they knew better as it was probably cloaked to prying eyes from above.

Mathew pushed the intercom button on his desk. "Ellen, please come inside the office right now." Mathew said, but the receptionist took a second to reply, having never to receive a verbal instruction through Mathew's channel. "Yes, Sir."

Without delay, Ellen entered the office with the two investigators moving closer to the desk and making a path for her to pass through.

Valerie looked at Mathew, but kept quiet.

"Alex, I need you to take our guys and move all of the investigators to the emergency centers. Screen everyone with blood and DNA testers. All of the other people not on duty will be given a month's vacation. Tell them to lay low and do not contact anyone. Ellen, tell the department heads the same thing. Once you have notified them, call Vicky, she will take you home. It is important you all watch your back and just disappear for thirty days. We will contact you if we want you to come in to work or have some other task, but if you are told to come in before the thirty days, do not. I repeat do not do so, even if you are sure it's me, Loren, Vicky, Kenji or Robert. Don't tell your family where you are going, just go and only use cash. Vicky will give you money if you need it before she leaves you. If you go see your family, stay with them or take them with you. Do you understand?" Mathew looked at her concerned face and then at the three men.

"Is there another copy of this?" Mathew pointed at the data stick.

"Yes Sir, at the center."

"Format all of the drives with it, delete everything on the servers and destroy any paper copies. Loren will go with you to the center."

"I hope you know what you're doing." Valerie said as she led the three investigators to the helipad. "Get back as soon as possible.

"Oh, Ellen, keep the doors open and come back here once you have verbally notified everyone." Mathew said and then called the rest of the guild.

It took Ellen a long hour to notify all of the department heads and direct staff to the owners. In the interim, the other four guild members arrived bypassing the ground entrance coming in the office from the helipad elevator.

"What's going on?" Lee asked seeing an empty reception's desk and Ellen nervously sitting on Mathew's sofa.

"Vicky, I need you to take Ellen home. Give her whatever amount of cash that she needs and make sure she gets off on her vacation before you return here." Mathew gave her a note with instructions. "Destroy this when you're done reading it."

"I will." Diana replied.

Once the two women left, Mathew turned to the three and showed them what Alex reported. "One of our teams in Africa found this base. Chances are that they know the corporation is behind it. So they might be coming here or will be trying to infiltrate us. I sent everyone home on a month's vacation."

"Everyone?" Cynthia asked.

"Everyone, except Alex and his teams. They are moving to our emergency centers. Valerie is escorting them back. As you saw Diana is protecting Ellen. We can't escort everyone around places so I thought it best to give people an early Christmas." Mathew slowly paced out in front of his desk.

"I guess we don't need to sign anymore either?" Kyle commented.

"No, it doesn't matter anymore. It's time we make our presence known."

"Darn, and I thought I was going to Fiji for a month." Lee grinned from ear to ear.

"Sorry my friend. You and Kyle will need to go destroy the base. The rest of us will hold down the fort and try to make sure there are no other sites and if there are attempts against use, they will fail."

"So you got rid of collateral damage or ways for them to use hostages. Kyle will get me there undetected and I will burn the place down." Lee summarized for the sake of Kyle's curiosity.

"So what are you two waiting for?" Cynthia asked as she got comfortable on the sofa.

Kyle sternly stared at her silently grinding his teeth. Lee walked next to him, leaning in by his ear and whispered. "Did you two get into a fight already?"

Kyle quickly turned his eyes to him. "No... it's just one of those mood things."

"No, it's not." Cynthia snapped from across the very large office.

Kyle grabbed Lee's arm and they both disappeared. "I love you baby." Kyle's voice trailed outside.

Cynthia turned away breathing slowly.

Mathew sat in his chair eyeing her antsy attempt to relax. "When are you going to tell him you're pregnant?"

Cynthia quickly locked onto his stare. "How do you know I didn't tell him... wait, how do you know I'm pregnant?"

"I'm not going to tell how I know your one week condition, but I will tell you if Kyle knew; he would have been so happy that no matter what your moods swings were, it wouldn't have bothered him one bit."

Cynthia breathed easier, delicately stroking her belly in thought. "You think so?"

"Did I miss something?" Diana entered the office through the ceiling, something the group was used to.

"No, Auntie Diana, you didn't miss a thing." Mathew smiled as he formatted his computer.

Lee and Kyle flew above the Sahara desert in northern Niger shortly afterwards. The morning sun hit with blistering heat, a drastic contrast to the cold nights. Once again Lee, wasn't able to see the cloaking energy field until he came up close on top of the coordinates Mathew gave him. The two men flew through the force field without issue. Lee scanned the area. Foot patrols were out this time. The androids were not disguised as normal human Soldiers in body armor. Their sleek weapons were attached to their right arms and large gear like shoulder pads gave them an intimidating flare. A cover with one inch horizontal bands replaced where a nose and mouth would exist. Lee could tell the metallic material in these machines were slightly different, seeming stronger than the malleable forms of the past androids.

"These guys are different." Lee whispered.

"Different? How?"

"We'll find out." Lee flew closer and higher.

One of the androids closest to them turned in their direction. Lee stopped flying and targeted the android's head from almost a mile away. The android walked a few paces towards them and stopped. He turned his head a few millimeters from side to side. Lee saw the difference with his optics and concluded the possibility the android was scanning the area with only needing to somewhat move its exponentially wide view receptors in his head.

With a quick about face the android returned to his designated route. Lee stayed at the current altitude and distance. With one hand he signed to Kyle. The phantom appearance of Lee's body and hand was not easy for Kyle to see but he understood the message well enough.

Lee's optics and laser rifle went into maximum configuration. The base wasn't like the others; it held several hundred androids, along with an accelerator system aimed up at the sky. There was no wall surrounding it, but was set up more like a standard airfield with no runways in the middle of an isolated area.

Kyle held a hand on Lee's shoulder as Lee counted off with his left hand and a four foot long laser cannon coming out of his right forearm. Lee started at five extended fingers and thumb, ending with a closed fist. Kyle lifted his hand off Lee. In a millisecond, Lee grabbed his aiming arm with his free hand and fired bursts of laser beams into all of the androids on the outside of the complex, inside structures and into the ground. The four seconds of destruction reduced any activity above ground to eerie stillness. The sound of air either moving or instantly burning by the beams was wrenching to the skin. Two hundred androids teleporting out into the open added to popping of air particles, the majority assembling in the direction of Lee's attacks.

The sky was clear with distant light clouds, the androids scanning and firing at the origin of the beams. Physical rounds and laser pulses riddled the air almost collapsing the cloaking field in the background.

Lee's appearance and laser attacks from the opposite side of the complex a mile out diverted all attention. A hundred seventy androids either exploded or were cut in half before any retaliatory fire headed towards Lee.

Lee disappeared, but so did the cloaking field. The morning heat moved in causing a massive gust of wind picking up sand several meters high. The androids ignored the sand screen as did Lee, while he fired from high up almost two miles out deep into the particle accelerator and remaining active androids.

Lee disappeared once again and moved east to a different

location. "Man can anything hurt you?" Kyle asked noticing several titanium rounds mushrooming on his energy suit before he turned him invisible and moved on, after the first attack.

"Yeah I got hit once in the leg a long time ago, but it wouldn't happen again." Lee scanned for any signs of activity.

"So why didn't you nuke this place like last time?"

"This place doesn't have nuclear chambers like the other one... But maybe that's." Lee pushed away from Kyle and fired a tight beam deep into the center of the complex.

Kyle turned visible thinking Lee was just cleaning stragglers. A warning alert popped up in Lee's visor. He instantly tackled Kyle and rapped his energy suit around him. An intense light erupted out of the ground pushing earth and air towards them. The mushroom cloud nipped at Lee's heels while in hypersonic flight away from the fission reaction. "I thought you couldn't do that!" Kyle yelled while thunderous rushing air and destruction reared its head.

"Why does everyone think I can control nuclear reactions?" Lee yelled back as they left the near ground level megaton explosion behind them, moving up into a low orbit back home.

Chapter Thirteen

Operation Pegasus

Southwestern Shore, Australia

R at Bastard watched and listened to the night critters and animals near and far from Alpha team three. Ghost's unexpected report caused the team to spring into action but in the opposite direction, "Where are you guys going?"

"We're going to clear a path and secure the exfil point. Can you help us run interference if we need it?" The female team leader asked.

"Of course." Rat Bastard smiled turning into the Rat and sped off along side of the point man who was bolting through the overgrowth.

Ghost saw the thoughts and understood the location would be vacant once he picked up team two. Spot was none too happy when Stargazer started his diversion, He wanted to let go of his grip between two Soldiers, but couldn't as Ghost flew outside into the morning night air. If he let go, he would have to physically penetrate solid ground and reinforced concrete to get close to helping his friend fight the androids.

"Drop us off here. I will fly the team to the extraction point, while you get the rest." Spot commanded.

"Good idea." Ghost replied audibly and mentally.

"Lieutenant Gomez, once Ghost drops us off, rope each other off so I can fly all of you above the trees." Spot continued.

"You heard Mr. Spot." Gomez authorized the action to the team.

The team materialized in a clearing. As soon as Ghost flew off, the team daisy chained themselves with mountain climbing D-rings and a forty foot nylon rope. Spot grabbed the center lifting the nine man team through the tree branches and bolted along the canopy short of a sonic boom towards the shore.

Stargazer pressed his jaw tighter as the deadly androids began to shoot various physical and energy projectiles at him. He swooped down onto a roll of androids, extending his right arm out. The impact of his arm was relentlessly consistent with piercing consequences. He learned his lesson from previous encounters. This time, his fist and forearm nicked eight androids on the chest, neck and head areas. He intentionally plowed into an android with a minigun, exactly like the one used in the Chicago airport assassination attempt.

The floor and capsules kept a number of androids from piling up on him, even though he was moving into the far end of the room. The impact of his body on the targeted android and chopping action of his left hand gave him access to the mini-gun's trigger. He collided along with four androids on the far wall crushing a metallic wall cabinet. The burst of armor penetrating energy bolts sprayed everywhere. Two android explosions from the initial strafing run were drowned out by the mini-gun's effects. The bolts almost melted through several inches of the androids' exoskeletons, before the androids in the facility effectively coordinated their attacks. To Stargazer's disappointment, the mini-gun was useless, being made to kill humans, not androids.

Two androids pinned him down against the wall as the other two yanked on his arms attempting to break them like they did on Spot. The expected broken bone results failed miserably as Stargazer focused on the other end of the room. The iron like grip of the androids on his wrists would be their undoing.

His strength was matched by theirs', but it didn't matter as two sonic booms shook the complex magnifying the shattering of glass within the enclosed space. His trajectory took him in a bouncing pattern from end to end of the center room and other adjacent rooms. The South American combat suit helped keep him decent, but it too was shredded to bits.

Ghost flew into the laboratory room Lt Chin's team was in, making himself visible to the team. "Nice." He exclaimed seeing two holes in the ceiling and two decapitated androids on the floor. The melted rough edges on the neck area of one of them were odd. An injured Soldier with a dislocated shoulder was being attended to by another near the body. The other seven Soldiers stayed close to each surrounding the injured man; all holding a saber handle in hand. Io was gone as far as he could tell.

"Let's go." Ghost grabbed the injured Soldier by his good hand and extended his other to the first Soldier to accept it. Within seconds Chin's team was moving out of the mountain facility. Stargazer's sonic booms shaking the room's foundation

Lt. Chin's team appeared in the same clearing less than a minute later, with Spot already waiting with a rope. There was no confusion to Spot's plan as Ghost immediately returned to get Stargazer with anxiety only knowing from Chin report that Io teleported out of the room once Ghost appeared.

Stargazer completed over a dozen back and forth devastating maneuvers. A dozen androids were out of commission, vaporized in their own self destruct programming or moving in for the kill.

Stargazer's momentum was suddenly hampered by the numerous small and large obstacles being thrown in his path.

An android finally laid a hand on Stargazer's head, releasing an intense telepathic paralyzing jolt. He tumbled aimlessly into a capsule. Five androids moved rapidly around Stargazer holding on to him, pulling him into a horizontal spread eagle position.

The other hundred androids stopped trying to fire on Stargazer and started to teleport out of the extensively damaged room as if their new task was to evacuate the area. The lights all throughout the complex turned off, emergency lighting taking its place. Only two lights were operational in the training room; one above Dr. Harlov's empty and wall-less office.

The five androids around Stargazer held him tight, scrutinizing him in the very dim light. It was uncommonly quiet as if the place was back to normal operations and the intruders were all destroyed.

The android holding Stargazer's head looked at him with a recognizing stare. He turned away into the darkness acknowledging another android. The tall masculine man walked up amongst the group taking over the task of holding Stargazer's unconscious head.

With one hand under Stargazer's sandy blonde hair, the Android lifted Stargazer's eyelid with his pointing finger. He used his thumb and index finger to keep the eye open as he maneuvered his pointing finger and touched Stargazer's pupil.

Light flared out the tip of his finger as if a laser cutter was being used to drill into Stargazer's brain. The other androids watched the procedure as Stargazer awoke out of his unconscious slumber. His other eye opening then slowly closing back up. He yelled and struggled but the androids restrained him. The emitted bluish white light stopped after a moment as did Stargazer's resistance. The android let go of Stargazer's head, letting it lifelessly hang down. None of the androids ever spoke, as was the case when the androids holding a limb let go of Stargazer's body. The thumping on hard metallic floor echoed throughout the room. The initial android that held Stargazer's head did not turn away, but looked at him intently. Then he turned his head at the executing android next to him. Instantly, the executor punched a spike into the android's nose area, using his own Tantalumized properties to find the physical and digital root self destruct command.

Stargazer sprang up and flew straight at a forty-five degree angle towards the outside near a closed ventilation duct, as Io teleported out of the room along with his fake executioner appearance.

Ghost was about to re-enter the mountain before Stargazer's thoughts hit him. 'Ghost I'm outside; go to the OBJ to link up.'

'Do you know where Io is?'

'Yeah, he teleported out already.'

'Okay.' Ghost replied flying into the OBJ where Stargazer was already waiting.

Ghost made Stargazer invisible but Stargazer was the one who propelled the pair super fast behind Lt. Gomez's team. Stargazer parted with Ghost and landed in front of the team. "All of you gather." Ghost appeared next to him.

The team held hands and the eleven people vanished to reappear at the exfil point three miles further. Stargazer surveyed the area, all personnel were accounted for, but he was looking for androids in disguise or pursuit. Five large hover crafts raced onto the shoreline remaining on the water, the Soldiers quickly jumping in and on the twenty foot sleek black crafts. The Five Ghosts stood with their backs to the crafts. "Tell the captain we will go home once we finish here. Thanks for the help." Stargazer yelled not having the ear piece anymore.

"You can't go back, if you do, you'll be killed." Chin replied taking the time to keep the last craft from departing.

"We have to finish the mission." Spot replied.

"Operation Pegasus is underway. We have incoming. Come with us or stay here for a few minutes to keep them from following us." Chin explained.

"We'll stay here until you're clear." Stargazer assured him.

Stargazer turned away facing the lowering tide, jungle and mountain in the distance. He quickly scanned the area again as far as he could, finding nothing. "Spot can you see anything?"

"No, there's no android in sight."

"Ghost did you locate Io?"

"No, but I know he's not in the mountain."

The sky above them illuminated with several hundred lights, disintegrating dark cumulus clouds, opening heaven. Millions of red and white light beams hit the mountain down to the base. The cracking of air was constant as if a lightning bolt never ended its shocking destruction. Stargazer looked up trying to find the source of the beams. Long drum like satellites in high orbit with large solar panels were firing at the mountain with impunity as the heat of the accelerated projectiles skewered and ionized all matter into vapor. The mountain looked as if it were digitized and was erased from top down in front of their eyes as a wave of hot burnt air spread past them.

"Holy crap." Rat Bastard said as he looked at his friends and then back at the empty space where the mountain used to exist.

"Yeah, that's some crazy weapon engineering... that's the

incoming Chin was talking about." Spot softly said.

"And to think the spaceships we were on could do something similar." Stargazer spoke out loud thinking of the destruction many races possessed but thankfully didn't use.

"At least it's cleaner than an A-bomb." Spot mumbled.

"The animals don't care about cleanliness." Rat faced him with tears rolling down his cheeks as the group stood in waist deep water.

"I found Io." Ghost excitedly announced pointing out at sea. "He's a mile out on the bottom of the seabed."

"Let's go get him and make sure the teams get to the ship." Stargazer's sadness remained as he placed a hand on Rat's shoulder empathizing with his goodhearted friend.

Spot flew into the water to retrieve Io after they arrived to the location Ghost sensed was correct.

As Spot returned Stargazer looked out to the horizon viewing the hovercrafts on hydrofoils linking up with their ship. The surfacing of four other ships in the area gave Stargazer an uneasy feeling. The South Americans were willing to get very close to land and with more than just one infiltration vessel. It was an easy way of instigating a war, if the hail of death from above hadn't done it already. He was expecting the Australian Air Force or shore batteries to start pounding the area, but for some unknown reason they seemed to be preoccupied or were being jammed somehow.

"The teams are okay, they'll be underwater soon. Oh and thank you for the micro message on your finger, it was quick thinking to be able to wake me up without suspicion." Stargazer reported and turned a thankful glare at Io.

"That is what heroes do." Io looked at Ghost for a reaction; Ghost nodding with approval.

The distant landmass was barely visible with lights giving it some shape. Stargazer could see aerial vehicles moving about and they would have all the reason to retaliate. But the scope of the incident was too big to give it a propaganda spin and what he feared now was the war which he though could be avoided was far from gone.

"Where to now?" Spot asked.

Stargazer solemnly looked at the men with a sense of lost hope as they floated a few feet above the waves. "We go home."

'So where exactly is home?' Ghost asked wondering what else they were supposed to do, now that the assassinations were either completely stopped or would escalate.

"Cassandra never said that stopping the assassinations would bring peace to the world. So for now, we find Master and have another group meeting." Stargazer said not wanting to declare a home just yet.

"Why were you expecting peace to be obtained when the android mission was neutralized?" Io turned a glare at all of the men.

"We had memories of this time period placed in our heads. So we sort of know the future." Ghost replied.

"More like visions." Rat Bastard corrected.

"Yeah, and some of those visions haven't come true. So, we're far from done." Stargazer watched the South American ships move back into the protective cover of water.

"According to the information I have gathered, the Australian government will stop at nothing to achieve world domination, as will South America. Whoever takes control of the world will be able to achieve a strong semblance of peace." Io changed into a backpack again as the group formed up to start their trip to Florida.

"Well, it's more complicated than that." Ghost replied.

Stargazer placed Io on his back. "What is making it more complicated than one ruling government?" Io's voice came out of the backpack as if it were a music box.

"It's complicated because of people like Cyer, Quatris and all those aliens we haven't met yet." Stargazer shot up with several sonic booms marking his fleeing presence.

Chapter Fourteen

••◆••

What Now?

T he morning came quickly as Mathew looked out across the magnificent history of constructed buildings professing a unified effort by people of many religious and ethnic backgrounds. He grew up as a superhuman with many abilities, able to create the entire city by himself if he had the time and know how. But it wasn't about him or the five superhumans relaxing in the next room down or working on laptops in his office.

He breathed deep as he thought about Lee's story on the Niger base. The nuclear signature caused an upheaval of news reporting to include severe allegations of the government conducting illegal nuclear weapon testing. That didn't trouble him though. The African Union was used to having telepathic investigators and courts. The truth of the matter would be the government wasn't involved and if they were, Australia would not allow such a secret to become fact or even rumored. What bothered him most was the large number of androids at the location which couldn't have been an increase in security, at least not that soon after losing the base in Antarctica. His folded arms made him look like he was guarding the city through the wall size window instead of just mediating on the next move.

Valerie typed emails to business owners and managers, making sure people weren't left in the wind because they had to lay low for a while. The legitimate businesses had to continue to keep livelihoods and families from becoming homeless or economically distressed. But her attention moved to her tall handsome black haired husband. His white dress shirt was almost spotless, considering he never sweat, but if there were stains or patches of dirt, it would have been due to things he rubbed on or touched. "Mat, what's bothering you?"

Mathew stared forward seeing the sunrise with extreme clarity. "We have a big bullseye on our backs."

Valerie stood up and moved out from Mathew's desk. "Maybe it's time we talked about what our next move is."

Mathew turned around facing her. The red glow behind him seemed to have given him a glorious aura of righteous authority. "Yeah, let's get everyone in here."

Valerie didn't know what to say for an unguarded moment. "Yeah, you're right." She walked up to the sofa and lightly tapped Cynthia on the shoulder. "Cynthia, can you please go get everyone so we can have a meeting."

Cynthia's hair moved aside as she straightened her head upright opening them wide. Her eyes were alert, but her voice said otherwise. "Why do I have to go wake them up?"

"Because my dear sweetie, you still haven't told Kyle, he's a father.

And if you keep insisting on the foolish worrying about his safety around you. I will treat you like my friend who needs a kick in the butt."

"If you were a real friend, you would let me tell him in my own time." Cynthia sat up and waved her hand. Several pulses of green energy came out of her fingertips hitting the wall by the entrance. The resounding bangs from the wall made it seem like the floor was under attack from with several grenades. "They'll be here soon." Cynthia smiled and laid her head back down.

Valerie bit her lip shifting her frown at Mathew. Mathew saw her rise in blood pressure and moved towards her. Valerie quickly moved next to him. 'And this is why I don't want to get pregnant.' She angrily signed in his face.

"But I would love it if you acted like that." Mathew smiled and hugged her.

"What?" She pushed him away for a second to see his eyes.

"Yeah, I would love it knowing you're moody because of a miracle. Even Cynthia will come to understand that."

Lee and Diana flew into the room, but they seemed to have figured out there was no threat in the area. Kyle appeared in the office as well next to the sofa above Cynthia. "What happened?"

"Cynthia has a life changing announcement to make." Mathew said as he guided Valerie to another sofa on the opposite side of the long coffee table.

Cynthia opened her eyes springing up sitting with a death stare on Mathew's dark eyes. "Why..."

"It's the right time and a real friend will always make you do the right thing, especially if it's good news." Mathew's tone was stern, but soft.

Valerie smiled as she sat down next to Mathew. "Kyle, why don't you sit next to Cynthia?"

Kyle's confused expression was shifting from being completely lost to worry. "What's going on?" He stared into Cynthia's eyes.

Her struggle to respond faded as she dug deep and held her head high. "I'm sorry for being so mean to you... but"

"It's okay darling, I can be your punching bag anytime you like."

"No honey, what you need to be, is a good husband and father."

"Well I'm working on that."

Cynthia smiled. "I'm pregnant."

Kyle's mouth opened but nothing came out for a second or so. "You're pregnant?" he smiled.

Cynthia returned the smile. "Yes, I'm pregnant."

Kyle joyfully hugged her and kissed her several times, as the rest of the group congratulated them.

"So do you know if it's a boy or girl?" Valerie said, the couple looking at Mathew for an answer.

"I know you might think I have some spiritual or supernatural power to know everything, but I don't. Besides, Lee knows."

Lee looked at Mathew with a dumbfounded sigh. "Why would I know the gender?"

"Because you can see it with those crazy optics of yours and already have." Mathew's gambler face dwarfed the confidence of his accusation.

Lee turned his stare at the couple. "Do you guys want to know?"

"It's not like she can go into a hospital and get checked out." Kyle replied.

"Actually we can, but it's a girl." Lee smiled.

"How long have you known?" Valerie asked.

"After we got back."

"Diana, you let him look inside of Cynthia?" Valerie's jaw dropped.

"She made me do it; otherwise I would be sleeping on the sofa for a week." Lee smiled as he sat on the love seat.

"I did no such thing." Diana objected.

"In the end, extortion never works like you want it to." Lee comfortably sat leaving a space for Diana to join him.

"Hmm." Diana kept her lips straight as she sat next to him in submission.

The sun shone into the office adding to the brightening mood.

Mathew let the group enjoy the moment before going over the options to their problem.

The top eight floors were vacant and quite, a normal day on a highly celebrated holiday, but this today wasn't normal or festive. Lee's sensors bypassed all security sensibilities which the group trusted. Not to mention Mathew's uncanny ability to see danger approaching.

Mathew placed two laptops back to back on the coffee table, while everyone moved to be able to see the screens. "As you know, our people are still looking out for more bases. Chances are they won't find anymore. The Australians also probably know we're behind them losing two of their bases. We can wait here and see if they attack us, move somewhere else safer and wait for them to attack us or we attack them." Mathew casually suggested.

"Since when did we start fighting a war against an entire nation?" Kyle asked.

"Since we killed Lanhurst, blew up two military facilities, killed a spy, since we went hunting for a reason to get leverage... do I need to go on?" Mathew ran down the list as he pulled up an image of Apex, the new Australian capital.

"We can get help from Creator and SIA." Lee suggested.

"I don't think they have our shoot first ask questions later attitude." Cynthia said, having become a mercenary because of bad court rulings and prejudice superhuman ideology.

"There might be a way. We don't have to make a pack with other people, all we have to do is get everyone to the same place at the right time." Mathew zoomed out of the city image displaying it as a small dot in the center of the continent."

"Well I can get a message to Creator, he might or might not pass it down to EFL, SIA or other superhumans willing to fight. But that doesn't help if none of the countries around the world, besides South America, will be okay with it."

"We need evidence people will believe of what Australia is doing on a large scale." Diana stated.

"Problem is all the evidence seems to explode in a big ass fire ball." Kyle sighed.

"I don't know my own strength." Lee smirked.

"That's a good thing, but evidence won't help anything right now. Let's say the whole world believes that Australia has created super machines being used to terrorize countries, kill off people that get in their way and most importantly have weapons that can cripple any nuclear exchange a stalemate. And on top of that, what do you think will happen then?" Mathew calmly hypothesized.

"World war three." Valerie softly replied.

"I have been thinking about something." Kyle muttered.

Lee smiled. "I don't know how to reply to that."

"No, I mean, we have been looking at this the wrong way. I understand how South America became a super power, but for Varken to come up with all those supporters and technology. Even though they have a shit load of superhumans, that doesn't account for the high tech that rivals South America."

"What does their technology have to do with it?" Lee countered.

"He's saying its technology not from Earth." Mathew stated.

"So we have aliens supplying countries with tech? For what?" Diana asked.

"To keep us in balance, to keep us fighting each other. Who knows?" Kyle suggested.

"If we don't annihilate each other, all it will do is weed out the weak and make it harder for aliens to take over if that's their end goal."

Mathew logically concluded.

"Okay, let's assume there is some ET influence, how do we confirm that and how is that going to change things." Cynthia asked looking at Mathew.

"If we have enough eyes looking out for the aliens, it might change things for the better."

"What if there are no aliens?" Lee asked, knowing superhumans were very well capable of boosting technology as well as chaos.

"Then we hope the good guys win the war. It seems SIA and their superhero groups are giving the androids a run for their money. But the longer we sit here, the higher a chance they will organize and try to take us out. So I need answer. Do we have a preference on the options I mentioned?"

"Yeah, I say we all take that vacation to Fiji." Lee leaned forward from his sitting position; his energy suit appeared around his hand as he touched one of the laptops. A satellite image of Fiji islands and distance to Australia filled the screen.

"I always wanted a command center above crystal clear water." Valerie smiled.

"Let's take all the gear we need for comms. The faster the better so is thirty minutes enough time?" Mathew looked around to all the faces.

"Yeah, Valerie and I can get the gear; you guys can clean the offices so they can't track us or the investigators." Lee said as everyone nodded in agreement.

Chapter Fifteen

♦♦◆♦♦

A New Age

Octavian Farm, Ft Lauderdale, Florida

Overdue piles of hay tumbled down the barn attic into a wagon below. Master watched the workers from a distance. The Octavian farm house reminded him of his dead family before his ex-foster parents forced him to move to the city. He missed the days of ignorance, but he thanked his new family for a life of knowledge. The Eternal Domain with Erica's insane communications capabilities made things a lot easier. He was able to focus on collating information and finding it, rather than hacking into everything with the risk of being found out. He slowly ate a turkey sub and chips on the patio. The noon sun was tempered with winter weather, but it was still warm enough for refreshing lemonade.

Cindy sat next to the teenager. Her perfect golden short hair flowed into a well kept bundle in the back. Her stylish pink shirt and jeans extenuated her comfortable mood. "So Erica tells me you're over fifty years old. How did you end up with here?"

"Kind of like your story I guess." Master shyly replied.

"My parents were murdered before I was able to get a driver's license. I was experimented on before everyone I knew and loved was killed. I ended up toppling a government agency by killing over four dozen people and then I met Richard who gave me a reason to change how I do things."

Master's awe wasn't as strong as expected. Cindy saw a loss he had kept inside, something she was very familiar with.

"Well, if you put it that way, your story sounds like a real comeback." Master stopped eating and faced his chair in her direction.

"My parents died in a car accident. Or maybe not so much being my dad was the drunk driver. My foster parents saw that I could make them a lot of money, so they played the Derby and other not so popular scenes. They mixed in with the wrong crowd. The good thing was they didn't expose me for my genius mathematical skills. They were murdered and I ran away. Gus found me in the streets of Chicago. We did well for a while. He was my bodyguard and parental authority as my dad. I was the bread winner with stocks and all. We were doing well for ourselves, but Gus wanted to help people, people we didn't know."

Master half laughed with joy. "I guess the big guy showed me it was good to care for people. Then Cassandra came into our lives. We found the island she told us to go to and there we met the rest of the gang. I killed I don't know, over a thousand people I suppose." Master looked down at the sub and took another bite.

Cindy kept quiet but leaned forward a little in anticipation.

"Well, I guess they weren't humans, but they were living beings, so I call them people. Yeah, well, we saved a galaxy. We could have gone home to my safe life, but we didn't and came here to fight these killing machines and the people running the show. So yeah, I guess that's a comeback story too."

Cindy smiled, stood and leaned forward, grabbing his head with both hands, kissing him in the forehead. "You're going to make some girl so happy one day."

Master's eyes lit up. "You really think so?"

"Yeah, but you might want to get started before you get too old." She smiled and drank her glass of lemonade.

"Now I know why Gus hits on all the girls."

"Well, his tactics aren't very effective in finding a nice girl."

"Finding has never been the issue, it's keeping them." Master finished his sub.

"Well, I think you won't have that problem. But what about the rest of the guys? What's the plan once your mission is over?"

"I don't know? We might be able to go back to our time or go back to Andromeda and stay with Cassandra. I know Spot and Ghost would like to go back there."

"What about you, Gus and Stargazer?"

"I'm not sure yet. It all depends on how everything works out. If I have to stay here in this time period, I'm okay with it as long as Gus is around and maybe I can make some new friends too."

"I've learned that we make our destiny to a point. Joshua will make sure no matter what you decide on, it will be okay." Cindy moved her chair facing the open pasture where five horses freely roamed.

"Who's Joshua?"

Cindy curled a corner of her mouth. "He's a super being that's keeping this world from total destruction."

"Well, if you see or hear from him anytime soon, tell him Niger would disagree with you."

"Hmm, people die all the time, but I don't think anyone died in that area. CNN said it was nuclear testing and Erica said it was an unpopulated area, even though there might have been a military base of some kind."

"The fallout will be felt in surrounding cities many years from now." Master stood up and stretched his arms above his head. "I understand that a super being can't control everything, otherwise there would be no free choice... but it would be nice to have a forceful reminder every now and then... Sorry I can't stay longer to talk, but I have to get back and see if Erica found out some new information."

"I'll see you down there soon." Cindy watched Master go inside the main house and into the distant elevator. "You really are older than you look." She whispered with a smile.

A large SUV approached the house that evening with Stargazer and the rest of the group unloading baggage. Richard and Master were the two to spearhead the introductions. 'What's in the bags?' Master asked Ghost as the men moved the bags to the main living room. The staff was introduced and the men were given rooms on the second story doubling up.

'It's for appearance. Creator wanted the location to remain a secret. The staff would question any sudden appearance of people from nowhere. But there's more than you know, but we'll talk about it in the open soon.' Was Ghost's reply.

The time came when Richard assembled all of them, with Larcis and Cindy present. Elizabeth and their son were out on an errand.

"As you can tell, I'm risking the identity of my family and this place to you. Max told me I shouldn't but it's time we have some form of trust before anything worthwhile can occur. Benjamin has been speaking with what He and Erica believe is South America."

"Benjamin? You told them your birth name?" Stargazer calmly said turning a momentary look at the teenager.

"Well, I couldn't have everyone call me Master. That would be very egotistical and rude, besides all of you used your real names with the staff." Master's humility was unchanged.

"Yes, I suppose." Stargazer smiled.

"You don't have to worry about things like that here. The staff are all screened and they won't attract attention. But to get back on the subject; if you are not aware of world events, two nuclear bombs have gone off in Niger and Antarctica in the past three days. Our sources say they were Australian bases housing a military capability. In addition, your escapade in Australia has made them declare war with Japan."

"What? Why would they do that?" Rat Bastard asked.

"Because they have apparent evidence that a Japanese cruise missile made its way into shore, but Erica will explain it better." Richard stood in the middle of the family room while everyone else sat all around.

"Orbital systems were re-tasked by all countries with satellite capabilities ever since South America became one nation. This limited the surveillance of South America and unfortunately, many other countries. Satellites used for surveillance or mapping started to disappear. Since South America has the market on satellite surveillance, they would have to expose the allegation which at this point they are probably debating." Erica's hologram floated in the air in front of the television screen.

"I disagree." Stargazer interrupted.

All eyes went to Stargazer wearing a Star Wars shirt and jeans. "It's all a smoke screen. The South Americans are ready to go to war. It wasn't an accident or coincidence there were probably over a dozen warships within five hundred miles of Australia."

"That's normal for how they operate." Larcis stated having examined the South American order of battle.

"Is it normal that they use an orbital attack system just to destroy a manufacturing plant and not think there wouldn't be consequences?"

"They've had no problem with nuking a country in the past. But I see your point. So are both of them making up reasons to go to war?" Richard followed Stargazer's logic.

"Don't you find it weird that EFL is pro South American?"

Richard smiled with crossed arms. "What I find weird is they haven't bought property there."

"So you know?" Stargazer asked as if it was a complete surprise.

"What I know is South America has not once acted like a villain. And if EFL wants to trust them, they can and honestly no one is going to force them to do something they don't want to do. I have learned to trust my friends and heroes. South America was united by a war. If they want to attack Australia, then I'm going to help them. But what you all don't know is there is more to it than South America or Australia. Knowing about your space adventures, you know aliens do exist. And it so happens that two of our members are now king and queen of the largest empire in this galaxy. They are I hope putting this galaxy in order and in case they for some reason fail, we will have to worry about an alien invasion, which is probably worse, than a world war."

"Who said anything about a world war?" Cindy said in alarm.

"I think it was implied." Larcis padded Cindy's hand with his.

Cindy looked around. "Yeah, it was implied." Master nodded.

"The question is who do we fight with and how do we help the situation instead of making it worse?" Stargazer stated.

Richard turned around looking at people. "Do you have any suggestions?" He stopped when he faced Io.

"If a war commences and we side with South America, I recommend we attack Apex and limit the deaths, but it is very likely all of the Tantalumized androids will be used for its defence. If we side with Australia, South America has created a dispersed command and control apparatus and eliminating one or two of the council members will only piss them off. Attacking Bogota will not change anything since we would have to take the entire continent to achieve a substantial victory. This will be very difficult because EFL will fight against us to include an estimated ten million Soldier military with probably the most advanced technology to date." Io's logic impressed even Erica.

"Piss them off?... you took the words right out of my mouth." Richard smiled.

"What's Apex?" Rat Bastard asked.

"Apex is the current capital of Australia." Erica replied.

"Oh... how much things have changed" Rat Bastard sighed.

"So what do we do for now? Just wait around until things hit the fan." Spot exclaimed.

"Androids seem to be causing problems in Africa, probably a reaction to get rid of witnesses. SIA did a good job in convincing other nations to hide their leaders and establish resources to keep law and order without having to enact Martial Law. Larcis, Cindy and I will go see what we can do. You are welcome to stay here, if you're needed, Erica will be one of the best sources of intel. I do recommend Io come with me. He limits your ability to be stealthy. Cindy can screen us and he will be of help against the androids."

"I'm okay with that plan if you are?" Stargazer turned to Io.

"I will do what I can to help." Io said without delay.

"If a war does start while we're gone, I recommend you move your team to South Korea, Erica will give you an address there. If we get split up I have a feeling we will need to be near Australia."

"Why are you so sure the Australians are the enemy?" Stargazer asked.

Richard faced him unfolding his arms. "If you were a good guy, why would you create an army of cold blooded assassins and pretend you are innocent? I told my guys a long time ago if you make an army it's usually because you plan on using it someway, somehow. South America has their army and so does Australia. They both might be bad guys, but so far only Australia has tried to kill innocent people."

"Hmm, since you put it that way, I would agree with you."

Richard stared into his eyes. "Steve, don't doubt your gut or your compassion."

Stargazer smiled. "Gina would have liked you a lot."

Richard returned the smile. "Yeah, Max told me that once."

The farm was quiet with Richard gone, but it was very active in the lower levels. Spot and Rat Bastard enjoyed the danger room, while Stargazer and Elizabeth enjoyed talking together and babysitting Richard Junior. Master and Ghost stayed in the battle room monitoring world events and Creator's progress.

It didn't take long for Master to link Operation Pegasus with Pegasus Prime. There was no direct link between the two, but information Master gave Pegasus Prime transferred to the group's visit in Bogota and with the mission.

"I still don't see how you see a link?" Ghost said after reading Master's findings.

"I will have to agree with Ghost on this one." Erica conferred.

"I'm telling you that the reason they started calling you the Five Ghosts is because I told Prime. And I'm sure that Pegasus is the name of the network of satellites, so hence Prime is someone with South America using the system calling himself Prime." Master proudly explained.

"The South American telepaths could have gotten all of the information you mentioned. Their satellite network is not a secret and the use of Pegasus was just a coincidence." Ghost insisted.

"Aarghh..." Master heavily sighed.

"Why does it matter if Pegasus Prime is directly linked to South America anyways." Erica asked as if she had no logics programming.

"Because, it means I will have a direct link to South America."

"You know that only works if they pay attention to you." Erica's sarcastic, sexy voice was enjoyable to hear.

Master laughed. "You're just jealous Prime can hide from you."

"Jealousy would imply I'm emotionally challenged and I assure you if I really want to find Prime, I would."

"So you don't want to locate a super hacker who can cause a lot of harm if he wanted to?"

"First of all, it could be a she. And knowing the location of Prime will only confirm a location, not a character we can trust."

"Okay, you're right Erica. We only need to know if Prime can be trusted. So why don't we give him a chance to prove himself?" Master sat on the leather sofa with his crossed hands above his head.

"What do you have in mind?" Erica asked as Ghost looked at the teenager. "Yeah, like what?"

"According to Cindy, the two nuclear explosions were two similar installations like in Bukkang going up in flames. This means that they lost three installations and one production facility; to include, most if not all of the assassins in North America. So why don't we ask Prime if he can confirm who took out those two sites and if South America will start a war?"

"What good would that do, Prime can lie his ass off." Ghost countered.

"Actually he can't because Cindy knows who took out those two sites and only Prime would know if South America was on the verge of starting a war. So if he lies, we will know." Master interlocked his fingers putting his elbows on the battle table.

Ghost looked at Erica's miniature holographic eyes. "There's a reason we call him Master."

"Yes, he's almost as smart as Richard." Erica's body disappeared and a large smile took its place for a few seconds and also disappeared.

'I really like these people... I'm glad Cassandra did what she did.' Master thought.

'Yeah, I like them too. And if I can't return to Cassandra, I wouldn't mind staying with people in this age.' Ghost telepathically replied.

"Okay, I guess a message is calling my name." Master set out to give Prime the request for information.

"Erica, you can come back now." Ghost said.

"I never left and I'll let you know when Prime replies. In the meantime I recommend you get some sleep and eat a well balanced meal in six hours." Her figure reappeared above the table.

The day passed with no reply and Stargazer along with Spot decided to take a tour of Miami. Crime was down and the economy was very stable for the moment with many early Christmas shoppers hitting the streets. The events outside of the states were quite different. Mideast tensions were increasing along with African incidents caused by nature and what the media now called Death Machines. Creator's international appearance was a surprise to many and a relief to several governments; except for North Korea who accused him for the death of three hundred people in the Bukkang province. Something they didn't declare until Creator made news in Libya. As usual, sanctions were not removed and Japan used an excuse to launch twelve additional naval vessels into the Sea of Japan. Spot monitored the events on one of Richard's modified comlinks.

"Man, these things are nice. I wish we had these when we were in Chicago." Spot said as Stargazer drove down Biscayne Boulevard.

"I think Richard is going to lose two comlinks once we get into a fight." He smiled knowing nothing they wore or held lasted for more than a few minutes in the heat of battle.

"Erica said it can handle like three thousand Kelvin temperatures and impact from a bulldozer." Spot looked at the small GPS readout indicating extras like altitude from the sea and to the ground.

"The wrist band will snap off once you punch someone."

"If you're so smart; how does Richard keep it from breaking?"

Stargazer almost laughed. "He's a shape shifter, he moves it into his wrist and his body protects it."

"What about Night, he can't do that."

"He shoots lightning bolts from a distance and doesn't try to hit anyone with it one."

"Hmm..." Spot thought about it for a moment. "Well, then I guess since you're the only one who plows through things, you should give me yours so I can have a backup."

"You know, that's not a bad idea. Comlink Stargazer remove from wrist." Stargazer spoke the command and the comlink's band released from the base dropping on the steering wheel and down towards the floor. He quickly snatched the comlink before it neared his knee and handed it to Spot. "Comlink Stargazer, transfer control to Spot."

"Thanks." Spot placed the band on his other wrist.

The pair drove around for hours, stopping here and there, ending up on the beach front that evening.

The city was so calm, something both men were not used to for almost half a year. However, Erica's alarmed voice scattered the schedule. "Ghosts we have a problem." Master's voice came on. "Guys, it has started. It's all over the news."

Spot held the comlink up, the small screen showed news reports of multiple rocket signatures coming out of South America. Stargazer instantly looked towards the southern hemisphere. "Holy crap." His tone perfectly duplicated Rat Bastard's previous shock.

"They have spaceships going into orbit." Stargazer zoomed in on the exhaust trails and up to the moving targets of booster assisted spaceships of various designs. If he hadn't seen science fiction shows in the past, he would have thought they were normal aliens. But he saw the similar designs of Star Trek federation and Klingon starships, Battle Star Galactica starships and very large cylinder shaped ships. He described them to Spot as they also watched Eduardo Ramerize on a live telecast on all channels declaring a new era for the human race. The clincher was the South American declaration of war on all countries of the world.

As soon as the broadcast ended loud sonic booms over the city rocked the sanity of all pedestrians and residents. Stargazer looked out towards the ocean seeing a large number of landing crafts south of them near Homestead. Hypersonic fighters flew north as if they owned the air.

"Reports are coming in that active missile silos are being attacked and anything military wise in the open is being lased in half." Master reported as it came into Erica's extensive communications network.

"I didn't see that coming." Spot breathed as if preparing for a workout.

"Yeah well, let's go pick up Ghost and Rat, and see if we can keep people from dying." Stargazer flew up and above the buildings followed by Spot, soaring into hypersonic speeds, causing added damage to glass windows below.

"Erica, get Ghost and Rat Bastard to meet us in the air above downtown." Spot spoke into the comlink.

"What are you guys going to do?" Erica replied as if they were up to no good.

"I don't know, I'm just following Star's lead."

Stargazer scanned far and wide. Patrick Air Force base was being overrun by ground troops, with not a fighter making it off the strip. He could only imagine how many bases near the water were totally taken by surprise. The amount of resources and coordination needed to attack the military sites and declare war on the world would've had to be unheard of; beyond enormous.

"These guys have been busy." Stargazer said under his breath.

The pair made it above Fort Lauderdale in minutes; Ghost and Rat meeting them with great anxiety.

"What do we do now?" Ghost asked as they floated in the air huddled in a circle.

"We can't fight the entire army." Rat exclaimed.

"They don't seem to be targeting civilians. Maybe they won't hurt anyone." Spot's hopeful denial came out.

"These US patriots are only doing their duty." Stargazer said as he thought about where to go.

"We can't police up the entire country." Ghost solemnly stated.

"I'm going to try, if that's okay with you?" Stargazer looked out to the north. "The military bases deeper inland will have more time to organize. They will have a higher risk of starting a firefight. So we go north, Fort Bragg or Benning. If there are no problems there, then we go deeper to Texas and Colorado" Stargazer extended his hand offering the rest to come along.

"Okay, let's go." Ghost made them invisible and intangible allowing them to proceed at full speed without attracting attention or inflicting auditory damage.

As the group flew north, Stargazer looked in all possible directions. Spot guided the flight path while Ghost displayed Stargazer's sightings to the entire group. "They are bypassing populated areas as much as possible." Stargazer said.

"They're using those satellite weapons to get rid of nuclear weapons and air defense systems." Ghost added.

"No, they're spaceships, not satellites." Stargazer looked up finding a similar Enterprise class starship firing its particle weapons down at targets somewhere in Europe.

"So that's what they had in the mountains." Spot surmised about Starfire saying they were next to a fortress.

"How many ships do you think they have?" Rat Bastard asked.

"A hundred, maybe more." Stargazer guessed.

"I wonder what everyone else is doing." Rat muttered.

"I don't think the comlinks work when we're intangible." Ghost commented.

"Give them a call when we stop." Stargazer instructed as he found a large amount of air assists moving west towards Fort Stewart Georgia. He changed course, monitoring the US Soldiers running through their war drills. But they were moving too slow, as if they were totally unaware of the approaching helicopters, with speeding tanks running down route 84. The South Americans were racing past cars and went off road just to get around traffic accidents and jams. A few police officers fired on the troops which clearly ignored their attempts to slow the invasion.

"I think all cell phones and other comms are being jammed or something." Ghost theorized, seeing that the Soldiers of the 3rd mechanized infantry division were completely oblivious to the approaching ground threat.

"Okay, this base is too large for us to go as a group. Spot take the east. I will take the ammunition depot before moving to the north, Ghost take the south and Rat you have the west. Make the commanders know if they engage the oncoming troops and aircraft, they will lose." Stargazer soared closer to the fort.

"Hmm, they might think we're working with the South Americans if we do that." Spot objected.

"Take their weapons away if you have to. That's why I'm hitting the depots first." Stargazer let go of the group and bolted to the nearest depot just before training area A-5 and range control.

A company of Soldiers and government civilians rushed to place barriers around the depot as vehicles started to convoy into the distribution storage center. Bunkers with armed and posted Military Police watched over the transactions by units picking up their allotted munitions. Stargazer's sudden appearance from the sky warranted a dozen screams and training of weapon systems in his direction.

"Halt!" Was the main and coherent word conveyed by the alarmed men and women. "Identify yourself." Was the second most understood word.

Stargazer stood bare-chested, his Star Wars shirt having ripped off from the hypersonic bounce to Ft. Lauderdale. "I'm Stargazer a superhuman. A South American armor unit is about to hit the Fort. Who's in command here!"

A yell from a Soldier on top of a bunker mount turned most eyes to the sky. "Incoming!"

Stargazer also looked to the east as two forward swept winged South American fighters strafed the depot blessing everyone with unending ringing sensations. Stargazer watched the planes continue to wherever they were headed to, but he was sure they weren't turning back for another supersonic run. Soldiers who recomposed themselves fastest started to throw ammunition into Bradley's and trucks that were present. One of the Bradley vehicles started firing its 25mm guns at two helicopters moving close to the tree line on the horizon.

"Stop!" Stargazer yelled in vain as he flew at the large vehicle two bunkers down. The retaliatory missiles were on their way, but Stargazer was fast enough to put himself between them and the Soldiers manning the Bradley. He strained to slap one missile making it detonate on impact and knee the other. The penetrating and explosive effects of the deadly missiles didn't harm his almost invulnerable skin, but they did remove any semblance of jean material off his lower body.

Stargazer heard the 25mm guns starting to buzz again. He instantly flew backwards into the minigun causing it to rupture to pieces at the expelling end. The vehicle's main weapon was out of commission, but the frantic activity by the Soldiers alarmed him.

"Stop firing, they will kill you if you fire on them!" Stargazer's loud words were deafen by the small arms fire , screaming of Soldiers as gun fire from the gunships sprayed concentrations of hostilities.

To his dismay, Stargazer witnessed a claymore mine explode, spreading death in all directions. The detonation of the mine was a one in a million without a priming cap and a current, but somehow one of the mines was triggered among munitions on a 5-ton truck.

The helicopters stayed at a distance, making sure small arms fire was ineffective, or just maybe waiting for reinforcements.

Anger filled Stargazer as Soldiers laid dead, bleeding or dying from multiple injuries. The Kevlar and all the protective plating minimized the damage, but one life was one too many for him.

Without thinking, Stargazer locked on to the gunship on the right. He bolted hitting Mach 1 before making contact with the South American fiber-metallic alloy protecting the cockpit. His fists punched through the cockpit instantly killing the pilot, but it also forced his hands apart. His head continued forward along with the rest of his body. The helicopter caved in to a degree, but the engine block took on the task of defying Stargazer's super hard skull.

The helo crashed into a clump of trees, all the blades maintaining their shape and operating integrity unabated, cutting tree trunks as the hull pushed itself into pile of pine needles, debris and dirt. An uncanny lack of fire or explosions littered the scene as the other gunship hovered in an overwatch position waiting for reinforcements, watching Stargazer's naked still body; feet sticking out of the fuselage.

Ghost and Spot encountered less resistance, but the outcome was far from peaceful. The town of Hinesville saw South American tanks and armor personnel carriers breaking the 65 mile per hour speed limit driving past the main entrance vehicle check points and into the first barracks. US Soldiers with access to M4s and crew served machineguns fired upon the South American Soldiers who had already dismounted. Commands for a surrender came out of all the armored vehicles booming their resolve if the US Soldiers did not comply. Spot flew in the midst of the gun fire exchange. To his surprise the South American

Soldiers were using plastic bullets, some of which had a chemical inside them. If it wasn't for the white liquid on his clothing, he would have thought nothing of it, but his enhanced sense of smell told him it was a paralyzing agent. "Guys take away the weapons from the US Soldiers. The South Americans are trying to use none lethal ammunition." He spoke as his comlink relayed the message.

Rat Bastard acknowledged, as did Ghost, but a moment later Ghost asked the one question Spot never would have imagined.

"Spot, does Stargazer have a comlink?"

"No, I have his!" Spot rapidly said as he tore away or bent weapons from a squad on top of the roof. 5.56mm rounds hitting him in the process as the Soldiers counted him as a hostile.

Ghost desperately called out to Stargazer, but nothing was the reply. His concern for Stargazer was diverted to the company of US Soldiers holding down the MP station. Thirty minutes of disarming and moving to hot spots diffused the situation between the two fighting forces. Ghost knew what Spot and Rat Bastard were going through as he concentrated on their situation, now that the South American units were successfully disabling or destroying the military's ability to re-group and try an offensive counterattack with military grade capabilities. Ghost disappeared from everyone's sight and gathered Spot and Rat Bastard. Their visible presence constituted too many questions and added violence to fragile situation.

With urgency, the group looked for Stargazer, finding the consolidation of units in and around the munitions depots. "I don't see or smell anything." Spot said as they slowly flew above the heads of the South Americans segregating US Soldiers, weapons, ammunition and attending to all injured personnel.

"Can you read their minds?" Rat Bastard asked hoping to hear Ghost reply with a resounding yes.

Ghost focused on the people seeming to be leaders. "Not the South Americans."

"What? Is there a telepath around here?" Rat asked.

"No, all of them were given mental blocks somehow, or they were trained to innately resist... but our guys are different. Be quiet for a moment." Ghost glided around looking into minds. An assembly of Soldiers sitting along a slope prepared to be moved back to their unit's garrison locations stood out to his mental scan.

"That woman remembers Star flying in and telling everyone to not fire at the South Americans." Ghost hovered over Staff Sergeant Roman-Hains. He focused harder but the fear and reactive impulse to jump for cover and not get hit by a speeding bullet was all he could see once the missiles started flying. "Damn, she only remembers that much about him, the rest of the time she was helping others stay alive."

He continued on trying to read more minds, but either he was exhausted or as usual, his ability was failing on new minds.

"Aargh... he was here but I don't know what happened once he got here." Ghost's frustration was felt in their collective minds.

"It's alright Ghost. I'm sure Star can take care of himself." Spot said trying to comfort him and Rat.

"Why don't we turn visible and ask the South American Soldiers?"

"Well he's nowhere around here so they will probably say he flew off in a cardinal direction. Unless you think he got vaporized or someone took his body away." Spot sarcastically joked.

"Well, he probably flew that way." Rat said as he looked out to the northwest. "There's a bunch of knocked over trees way out there."

Spot looked in the specified direction, also dragging the group and flying to the location.

The toppling and breakage of a fifty meter strip of pine trees suggested a crash. An imprint of something heavy suggested something besides an unexploded ordinance failing to work properly. But the absence of an object on the disturbed ground meant whatever was there grew some wings and flew away. Unknown to the three men, another helo removed the wreckage with Stargazer still in it.

"We need to tell Erica and Richard what happened." Rat Bastard highly recommended.

The three men became tangible, but remained invisible to the naked eye. "Erica, can you hear me." Ghost asked not really comprehending how the comlink worked.

"I can now. May I ask why you're in Georgia at the moment?" Her seductive echoed voice sounded more domineering than inquisitive.

"We tried to keep the peace. But we lost Stargazer." Ghost replied raising his comlink to his mouth.

Spot grabbed Ghost's wrist and lowered his hand. "You don't need to do that, just talk."

"You're being too ambiguous. Do you mean Stargazer is dead?" Richard came on the line.

"No, we mean he's gone and we don't know where he went." Rat Bastard intervened.

Everyone didn't need enhanced hearing to hear Richard's heavy sigh. "Alright, we're on our way back to ED. You guys go back too and meet us there. Stargazer is a big boy. He will turn up. But for now, stay out of trouble and get back to Erica." Richard said as Night's hypersonic booster kicked into overdrive.

Spot touched Ghost's comlink. "We're on our way." A red light flashed.

"Okay, we can talk now without them hearing." Spot continued.

"How do you know?" Rat Bastard asked.

"Man, do you guys ever read the instruction books?" Spot was almost annoyed.

"No, they confuse me." Rat honesty was irreproachable.

Ghost smiled. "So what do we do?"

"Well, we can keep looking for Star, but it's going to be dark soon and we really have no idea where to go or where to start." Rat Bastard stated.

"I hate to agree with you, but unless we can find a clue very soon, we might have to go back to ED." Spot confessed.

"Okay, let's think about this. Stargazer has never been hurt except for the time in the mountain when he was unconscious from a hundred androids. I can't hear his thoughts, so he is either unconscious, I'm being messed with or he's too far from me to communicate with him." Ghost surmised.

"What are you talking about, you could sense his thoughts for several trillion miles when we were in Andromeda." Spot retorted.

"We were on a spaceship and being on a planet is different."

"After all this time, now you tell us." Rat Bastard frowned.

"Okay, whatever. Let's just go back to ED. Richard will have a plan and hopefully wherever Star is, he will find us." Spot recommended.

"You know. Every since we stopped bringing Master with us, things just don't work out very well." Rat Bastard said with raised invisible eyebrows.

"Yeah, it feels like it doesn't it." Spot said as he used his flight to take the group back to the Eternal Domain.

Chapter Sixteen

Tsunami

Savu Sau, Fiji Islands

B amboo ceiling stretched across the large arch. Dark rolling clouds kept the Sun at bay, but the touristy lighting in the room reflected the wood's clean exotic texture. The tropical shower gave the guild reason to stay indoors and people away from them. The open floor plan allowed them to appreciate a different scenery; at least for some.

"And I thought we were going to monitor a computer out by the waves." Diana's grumpy mood bounced off deaf ears.

"If you like, you can go lie by the beach, we'll let you know if something comes up." Mathew replied.

Diana's eyes tighten as she stared at him, then at Lee. "You know I think I will." She stood up and flew through the wall, phasing back to normal; casually walking straight for the shore.

"You know you pissed her off?" Lee said.

"No, you did for not sticking up for her." Mathew smiled as he browsed the investigator reporting and SIA intel feeds.

Valerie came in from one of four bedrooms. A large plate of partially missing sliced fruits and finger treats rested on her extended hand. She walked towards the men in the living room looking around expecting three people. "Here are some snacks. Where's D?" She placed the plate on the table next to Mathew's computer.

"She went to lie out on the beach." Mathew said.

"In the rain?" Valerie excitedly asked.

"Yelp, in the beating rain." Lee confirmed.

"Why didn't you get me." She snapped with joy and shrunk into speck size, flying out through the window mesh after Diana.

The two men silently looked at each other then focused back down at their computer screens. "And to think we were the ones wanting a vacation." Lee broke the silence.

Mathew smiled. "Next time, I come alone with Valerie, you guys can find another island."

"I totally agree." Lee satisfyingly munched on the treats. "Well I have nothing new for now."

Mathew scooted back away from the laptop. "Same here... hey I have an alert setup, so why don't we take the girls on a walk."

Lee smiled pointing a carrot stick at him. "By the beach?"

"In the rain." Mathew smiled.

Lee led the way out the sliding backdoor towards the shore. "Besides, Kyle and Cynthia can use the sleep so us being gone is a good thing."

The evening and night was well spent, as the group got time to relax and unwind.

But the morning came early and quickly as reports of a military strike in Tasmania Australia triggered the SIA alert with the investigating team confirming it.

The group gathered reading the news with interest. "Well we can assume someone else is trying to do some harm to Australia and if the targets are bases like the ones we hit, then we might have a chance." Kyle commented.

"This one is a little different. See this." Mathew pointed at a classified image of a mountain range. The angle and clarity was at best inferior quality, but it was a long range photo penetrating the atmosphere at a very drastic pitch. "You see that area there?" Mathew pointed at the outline of a low area as if sketching along the shoreline with a pencil.

"I don't see anything." Kyle said, everyone else agreeing.

Mathew took a second to breathe glancing at Lee. "You can't see that?"

Lee studied it a little slower and tilted his head. "Someone excavated the mountain."

"Old military photos say there used to be a three thousand foot mountain there."

"So they gutted it, so what?" Valerie remarked.

"Not in a week. And there's no debris, so something like a laser or disintegrating weapon took it out."

"As far as I know there are only a few people with that much power. Quatris and Hellfire are MIA and it would take me a minute or two of constant firing to do that." Lee said.

"It would drain you, too." Diana added.

"And since we all know it wasn't me, could Hellfire or Quatris be undercover or something?" Lee asked.

"I had a mission one time to destroy an oil tanker." Cynthia recounted the memory as everyone paid full attention. "I couldn't just sink it, I had to make sure it didn't spill, otherwise the insurance company would not have been able to cover it. Anyways, I could have blasted it from the sky and took my time burning the fuel before other ships arrived. But instead of taking the risk of my time being cut short or the oil spilling all at once... I chose to get a large team of pirate ships to take the ship. I took out the comms before they knew it and the pirates drained the tanks using twenty smaller ships as tankers. Then I blew it up after the crew were removed."

"That was the Exxon disaster in 04." Kyle recollected the news report. "That was you?"

"So what does that have to do with the mountain?" Diana asked.

"You're assuming it was one person, I say it was a lot of people or at least a lot of weapons." Cynthia proudly leaned back with a slight grin.

"And who has those people or weapons that can do that without getting caught?" Mathew opened it up for answers.

"Surely not Japan... So maybe SIA?" Kyle started to say.

"South America." Lee ended the list.

"But that wasn't an accelerator or force field device?" Valerie repositioned her long hair to her right shoulder front.

"So what was it?" Kyle doubted her claim.

"According to the data in Antarctica, the force field generator is supposed to combine with others to strengthen a field in the atmosphere. The accelerators go deep into the Earth and use the energy from the core, so being in a mountain will require they go deeper, which sort of defeats the purpose. Unless it was a volcano, which it wasn't." Lee explained.

"What if it was a test bed and being in the mountain would make it easier to hide if they started a long time ago." Cynthia became another devil's advocate.

"Whatever it was, it was out away from everything. There are a lot of mountains there, but it would have been easier and safer to create the device, if it was a device, in the center or near Apex. And..." Mathew paused in thought.

"And, what?" Valerie insisted.

"And if South America was behind this, it was important enough to reveal they have some serious capability normally reserved to rare superhumans like Lee." Mathew said as he went over specific data Lee mentioned.

'Why does it matter who attacked Australia; haven't we attacked them twice and SIA indirectly in North Korea?" Diana stated.

"I guess it really doesn't matter, but what if the Australians are making a force field to protect the planet from outer space?" Mathew theorized what seemed unlikely.

"Are we really talking about aliens again?" Valerie's scientific curiosity had her sit straight as if readying to ask questions.

"Just because Lee found some weird data bits doesn't mean they're alien?" Cynthia stated.

"I don't need proof, I know because my sister told me it was true that aliens exist. Quatris and Hellfire are well known for their absence in the middle of world crises because they're in space." Lee confidently looked at Cynthia.

"All of this sounds interesting, but putting a force field around the planet won't stop aliens forever. In fact, it sounds like a remake of a Highlander movie which almost destroyed the Earth if I recall correctly." Cynthia raised her eyebrows and crossed her arms.

"What's on your mind?" Valerie glared at Mathew waiting for him to look at her.

Mathew turned his head. His dark gray eyes seemed to have bore the weight of the world, but no more. "Diana and I were attacked because we were superhumans. Not because we were going to stop the Australians from creating a defensive weapon against an unknown enemy. The Eternal Champions seem to be fighting the same enemy. That enemy is Australia." Mathew calmly said as if giving a final speech to an audience of skeptics.

"We came here to be closer to Australia so now that we're here, what are we doing here?" Lee asked wanting someone to reinforce their earlier decisions.

"We're waiting for Alex to report there are no more bases or devices. One or two might escape their recon teams which has already covered most of the uncharted regions or possible areas that could be cloaked, but that's okay. What I want to do is gather information and make a plan on attacking Apex." Mathew said as he stood up and walked away from the group stopping short of the kitchen.

"Apex will be defended by those mechanical assassins; not to mention a hell of a lot of superhumans." Kyle stated as Mathew turned to face the group.

"Aliens too, if they're involved." Valerie added.

"What makes us strong is being a team. We need to just wait for the right moment." Mathew said, continuing his trip to the kitchen and opening the frig.

"Here on this island, live what; maybe eighty-thousand people? They see paradise, not really what the rest of the world worry about. But they do have the same cares to make a living, they try to live it as best they can, happy and safe. We should take the time to help them out by volunteering our time, expertise and money to give them a reason to have hope." Cynthia recommended.

"I'm confused, when did we change the subject?" Lee asked.

"I have seen you guys take the time to help people in the middle tornadoes. So instead of being glued to the computer screen, we should go see the natives and make some of their dreams come true, while we wait for the need to blow stuff up." Cynthia pointed at Mathew motioning him to bring some food she was now craving.

"That's my woman." Kyle proudly hugged and kissed her.

The others looked at each other in thought. "I can go talk to the mayors or the President." Valerie volunteered.

"We can go speak to major companies and charities." Cynthia added Kyle in the effort.

"Yeah, I'll go with Val."

"We can help the hospitals." Lee turned to Diana, her smile approving of his intentions.

"Okay, its settled then. Just make sure you keep your phones active and not the combat ear pieces. I will let you know if anything new pops up." Mathew gave Cynthia a bowl of fruits and honey.

The group's connections, money and expertise in business helped the local organizations in providing reduced or free services to the public. It wouldn't really be noticed for another several days to months, but the government and small businesses appreciated the unexpected visit by wealthy strangers.

Lee's optics and Diana's phasing ability helped surgeons with impossible feats that day. The stylish glasses Lee wore disguised his ability to see and project the information into a monitor, as well as Diana's delicate hand in removing foreign objects from tissue. But the next day brought a looming urgency for chaos to attract fear and reactive survival preparations as South America's worldwide broadcast in over four hundred languages took prime focus on all television channels. All satellite communication used by the military, SIA and other agencies were jammed or destroyed at the source. The six watched with wonder, even more so once Lee went outside and reconfigured his optics to search the skies. He linked into Mathew's laptop, showing everyone what he saw. The telescopic magnification was fantastic along with his tracking algorithms, but it was a big sky. The images of various starships and satellites indicated they were strategically positioning themselves to cover specific regions of the world. Site to site communications wasn't hampered, which helped reduce the commotion of chaos on the island. "What are we going to do now?" Lee asked, as he looked down and around the neighborhood.

People were either glued to the television, radio, calling people or moving about with an apocalyptic purpose. "How are we going to protect them all?" Lee continued to ask.

"We don't, for now we help the people on the island." Mathew replied with the group coming outside next to Lee.

The grass ended along the beach line twenty meters towards the west. Many people out in the water and on the sand were ignorant of the world changing event. South America had taken the initiative and now it was Australia's turn to perform something just as crazy.

"Okay, we go and help whoever; in getting to shelters, getting to locations inside the country, stop any looting and so on. Don't worry about concealing your superhuman abilities." Mathew said as Valerie waved her hand; five uniforms grew into existence.

All six split up into the corners of the island, assisting who they could. Mathew made sure he presented himself to the President and parliament members offering the team's capabilities. Lee's capability to use the repeaters and phone towers kept them informed on what each was doing to include any news from any source that made it to them. Alex's team was off-line, but Mathew knew he would figure out a way to get them intel from half way around the world. Cruise liners set out to sea, in hopes of getting people connected back home to families or at least away from a potential cross fire between the two superpowers.

It wasn't long before people who were going to stay for the long haul accepted their decision in hope of surviving and protecting their families and homes.

Several days passed as normal communication was permitted by South America's orbital and ground network. Alex provided intel, but it was in the clear and mostly confirmed the news reports of what was going on in the US, Europe, Asia and North Africa. Any news of Australian and South American encounters were either not reported on or non-existent. Mathew and Lee knew better. All nuclear and military installations in Asia were overrun or destroyed. Japan quickly sided with South America, but their surrender only kept large numbers of military assets from being used on the country. Two million South American ground troops consisting of two Mechanized Legions scattered throughout Asia, with most regions providing little resistance against the well organized and able forces.

Reports were similar in all other continents except for the Middle East. The South American 6th Armor Legion met extreme resistance in Egypt eastward to Jordan on the first three days of the war. Many countries criticizing South America's actions saw a glimmer of hope as the 3rd SOF Task Force held the legion at bay with substantial victories. The fourth day of victory went to South America as the 10th Armor Legion succeeded where the 6th failed. But the events were far from them and Mathew's focus was well warranted.

The team stayed in Fiji's emergency command center; now that the days of chaos were less chaotic. The Fiji military was small but perfect for maintaining order and essential services to the public. Reports of nearby naval activity caught everyone's interest.

"Mr. President, I recommend all personnel outside be moved to the shelters, as we discussed in case of fighting near the islands." Mathew warned the entire panel of leaders managing the country.

The President agreed and ordered the contingency to be executed.

Lee motioned to Diana while the order was given, and they both flew straight up out of the bunker. "Why did you want to come outside?" Diana asked as her molecular structure returned to a natural flesh and blood state.

"It's easier for me to see what's going on out there from here." Lee scanned the north and west horizons. The mountain bunker they occupied was well positioned for the crisis, but it only provided a good ground vantage point, not something Lee really needed.

"How far can you see"" Diana looked out; cloud cover giving the island and ocean scenery a beautiful appeal.

"From where we're standing, about two hundred miles with my radar, but only fifty miles for anything underwater... Tell the team to use our close quarter comms. I will boost the distance. In the meantime, I need to fly out and find out what might threaten the island. My radar will work bête at higher altitudes." Lee instructed.

"Why don't we wait? Mathew said we would join the South Americans once they move against the Aussies."

"I have a bad feeling. I love you my goddess." Lee passionately kissed her; his energy suit appeared and he flew off to the north.

A detailed 3D topographical image moved rapidly behind Lee as his helmet showed a sphere of analytic data in all corners of his eyes. His optics simultaneously tracked all possible threats and physical objects of importance according to his subconscious and perceived thoughts. Any foreign objects on or in the water would show up as markers along with statistical data of the asset.

Two minutes in the air, confirmed his fears. A Russian Borey class submarine was under attack by an Australian destroyer. Just outside of the two hundred miles, the destroyer had launched several torpedoes at the doomed vessel. The impact of one torpedo was the telling sign Lee had of the encounter. To his surprise an electromagnetic wave confirmed the readings his optics were giving him along with the temporary intense flash of light. "What the hell, that should not have happened." Lee told himself knowing the submarine's nuclear ballistic missiles would not explode while in the sub or during its travel until a specific time over target when it would arm itself.

The very large yield explosion lifted millions of metric tons of water less than a hundred miles from the islands. Lee witnessed the efficiency of South America's resolve as a tight energy beam from the sky hit the destroyer for a few seconds, cutting it in half. The distance to the destroyer made it hard for him to see in detail, but it wasn't hard to make out the ship breaking apart and almost instantly sinking like a brick. He was sure the hundred or so sailors on the ship had no chance, as did the one hundred and six submariners who were just entombed in a horrifying underwater death. The Russian submarine's depth read well below seven hundred meters before it was hit. There wouldn't be any nuclear fallout, but that was only one of numerous terrible effects.

"Mathew, there was a nuclear explosion, I'm estimating several megatons underwater. I'm not sure but it was deep and there might be a tsunami heading your way." He scanned the water, his optics adjusted to focus specifically on water temperatures and density.

Lee flew back towards the main island; the underwater shockwaves were on their way, giving the Fiji citizens and tourist about twenty minutes notice before possible disaster became reality.

"We'll prepare for the worse." Mathew replied.

Lee soared above the calm surface water. Many of the inhabitants near the shore were already evacuated since the days before, but their migration only took them several miles inland. A group of people posted themselves on top of the northern peak; a ten minute walk to the bunker. They held long range cameras and started to erect several tents. He wasn't sure if they were reporters or curious fools; but his concern focused along the structures near the shore. A substantial tsunami would flood the area with debris and unwanted force.

He flew down to a street corner watching a large wave move way above the breaking sand dunes. The rest of the group was already taking people away from the area up to higher ground. The rushing of water and debris slammed into miles of property and wildlife. "It's not enough!" Lee shouted. "The waves are going to pass the safe zones."

The single family huts didn't help the situation as structures, trees and automobiles trampled everything in its path. The group watched in despair as several hundreds of people were swallowed into the debris.

"Diana, Valerie, come with me so I can show you where there are survivors." Lee instructed as he flew over the area still covered with moving water.

The two women flew to his side and dove into the areas Lee pointed at. Dead and living were phased or instantly grew out into the open air. Kyle and Cynthia helped in transporting people to the nearest medical sites, but the blood, carnage and numbers of horrified faces made its mark.

The waves ebbed off with the water slowly receding. An hour into the rescue operation, the survivors were managing the crisis better than expected. The team flew back and forth moving debris or using their abilities to collect people.

President Losi gave his sincere thanks to the group. It was all he could offer as the death of over a thousand people along the islands' multiple coastlines was the greatest disaster to their country since 1970.

It was a short thank you as Mathew and the rest returned to recovery operations in restoring power and water to the areas they could best help in. Lee and Mathew quickly disabled downed power lines and moved large debris off of routes needed to get to remote locations.

The dryness and comfort of his suit was nagging at his subconscious. The time of immediate danger waned in the crisis; long enough for him to float above a sand and debris covered paved road. "Joshua... How can you let this continue?"

"If it were a tsunami caused by an earthquake, would it have justified their deaths?" Joshua's voice was audibly heard as clear as speakers glued to his ears; but what Lee didn't know was Mathew and the rest of the guild heard it as well.

Lee frowned with building anger. "We can go all day about cause and effect. You know you could have prevented all of this. Why does it have to be this way; when is all this killing going to stop?"

"Your presence and actions saved many people today. But as you have experienced, you can't save everyone." Joshua replied.

"Is this some kind of life's lesson?" Valerie asked; Lee looking around thinking she was next to him, but realized the group was included in the private conversation.

"No, it's very real which would have been worse if you had not been here." Joshua's voice was calm; almost like a father reassuring a daughter.

"Why is this world war necessary?" Lee reverted to the original question.

"People will always have some excuse to fight; now they will have a better reason to have peace. Not by the threat of war or destruction, but by the enforcement of truths." Joshua started to lecture.

"And what are those truths?" Diana asked.

"That your so called freedom and peace comes at a cost, which you and others like you will pay for. That we as a people must submit to each other, for the good of all." Joshua's voice trailed off in the distance.

After a moment of silence all of them asked questions, but it wasn't heard except by the person doing the questioning. Lee spoke on his head mic. "He's gone."

"Who is he?" Mathew asked what everyone else wanted to know.

"Joshua is the superhuman who saved me and my sister when we were teens. He is for all intensive purposes a god." Lee said as he flew to Mathew's location.

"Why didn't you mention him before?" Valerie curiously instead of accusingly asked.

"Joshua does what he wants, and as far as I know, he doesn't want worshippers."

"It doesn't matter who or what he does or doesn't do. We need to collect ourselves. Lee can you get your sister to arrange a meeting with Creator? It's time we headed to Apex. In the meantime, we will clean up around here." Mathew continued to move large structures making it easier for recovery personnel to put things back to normal.

"I will try. I will go make sure there aren't any more surprises coming this way." Lee replied and flew up and away making a circular route around the collective islands.

Chapter Seventeen

Sit and Relax

T he lower levels of the Eternal Doman were unusually populated by wide-eyed employees and neighbors. South American units bypassed all major populations, focusing on military and political targets. This fact didn't change Richard's decision to gather all the staff and any neighbors seeking shelter. It wasn't hard to go around the block telling everyone there was a bunker in the property, but no one expected to find the bunker was like a miniature super installation only seen on dramatic spy movies.

Everyone except Stargazer rallied in the battle room. Richard's trusted staff managed the new residents while the superheroes went over their options.

"It's been three days now." Richard stated while we watched the reporting coming from many sources, being collated by Erica.

"So what do we do now?" Rat Bastard asked hoping someone had a proactive plan to search for Stargazer.

"I studied Stargazer's unique body. Three days is a good sign that he's alive." Io stated while also analyzing the reports on the screen.

"He should have contacted us by now." Ghost countered.

"Considering Stargazer's invulnerability, it is highly unlikely he was killed or disintegrated. There is a slight probability he received a head injury and has amnesia or similar issue." Erica stated; her hologram floated above the battle room table.

"Or he could be with the South Americans helping them with the invasion." Master commented; Erica acknowledging the claim with a head nod seeing the data he just opened.

"What?" Spot asked almost standing up off one of several single chairs by the kitchen island counter.

"Pegasus Prime says Stargazer is safe and he will not be joining us at this time." Master replied as if giving a report to a teacher.

The group looked around the room in doubt.

"Okay, Prime has been accurate so far. Master, you stay here with the rest and hold the fort, Liz and Junior will also stay. The rest of us will go see if we can do something in Australia." Richard stated.

"South America seems to have things under control; we should help people around here." Night suggested.

"No, we need to go meet my brother, as soon as possible." Cindy interrupted with an insistence in her eyes.

"And where's that?" Richard asked.

"Fiji." Cindy said turning into her superhero costume.

"What about Starfire and Starlight?" Io asked fully knowing the danger of attacking Apex.

"Bob said they're busy at the moment, but will be there when we need them. Okay, say your goodbyes before we go, in case things go wrong. Be back here in five." Richard walked up to the elevator heading up to see Elizabeth and Junior.

UFSD Tarsus, three thousand mile orbit

Soft but resilient bands kept Stargazer fixed to a moving bed. His eyes slowly opened; escaping from a restful place his dreams wished he never left. The ceiling was well lit as if a thin LED strip ran down the six foot wide hallway. A lovely woman walked with him by his head, looking forward past his feet. Her white uniform resembled an expensive ski suit, but this one had sophisticated layers used to regulate extreme temperatures. He scanned through the ceiling penetrating several layers of alloys, ceramic, glass, magnets and compartments, then space. The stars were joyfully bright as he knew so well. The aligned constellation confirmed he wasn't in another galaxy, but it didn't mean he was on Earth either as the lack of strong gravity also felt so familiar. He picked up his dead seeing there were no others beside the woman pushing him down towards a turbo lift. It was not as large as the ones he was used to in Andromeda, but it was well constructed.

"Relax Mr. Stargazer we will be arriving in the bridge shortly." The woman said looking down at his sandy blonde hair.

Stargazer looked up a little to see the inside of a spacious bridge configuration similar to a Star Trek movie, minus the impractical transparent panel screens. The elevator door automatically opened, Stargazer could see cameras all around to include two in the elevator; probably used to activate doors and monitor access. They entered the elevator as the woman spoke. "Mr. Stargazer, I am going to lift the bed forward. Do not be afraid, once I release the straps, you will be able to stand. Do you understand?"

"Yes, it's okay." Stargazer replied; the woman lowered the bed at the feet and raised his head. The straps loosen and retracted into the six inch thick platform. The bed stood straight up, as the woman slide it aside next to the wall of the elevator. There were no wheels or legs on the bed, reminding him of the magnetic platform he stood on in the

Vorg Space Station. Stargazer's boots and pants pulled his body down against the floor creating a gravity effect.

He was wearing the same space suit as the woman, except his was grey in color. The woman also had a helmet attached to her side. The elevator doors slide close. "Bridge." She said and the elevator moved up one level and turned in place.

The doors slide open to reveal what he had already seen through the walls and floors; but didn't bother to look at faces. The woman remained in the elevator and disappeared with the magnetically balanced bed. His boots seemed to know when to attract to the floor and when to release.

"Welcome aboard Stargazer." Eduardo Ramerize sat in the captain's chair, centered in the oval room, his black space suit complemented the bridge crew uniforms. "I wish it would have been under better circumstances."

"You brought me into space?" Stargazer saw the Earth below on the main screen, not needing to peer through the ship.

"No, my guys brought you here; after you killed one of my pilots trying to disable a Bradley fighting vehicle." Eduardo got out of his chair and walked in front of him.

"If you think two missiles hitting the Bradley is disabling, I would disagree." He stared him in the eye; crossing his arms.

"The missiles would've hit a track and the gun. The crew inside were safe." Eduardo said with an extended open hand.

"Oh." Stargazer relaxed.

"There is no way we can keep everyone from dying, but I assure you, we are not bloodthirsty. Please, relax and you can decide for yourself." Eduardo withdrew his hand and motioned to an empty seat next to a console full of screens, buttons and dials.

"As you are aware, we have declared war on the world. We have been planning this for over four decades. Ships like this one are in a high orbit providing support to all ground, air and naval forces on the planet. Once we're done, there will be no more petty squabbles about land, politics, ethnic backgrounds, religious superiority or who's in charge. We have proven that many nations can come under one governing system and prosper with justice, fairness and peace." Eduardo stood next to him.

"You mean one system which you control?" Stargazer's candor cut to the chase.

"A system run by five council members and over four hundred representatives. But don't worry most current country leaders will remain in place. They will be part of the public's House of Representatives, and Councilmembers will run for office, the only difference is telepaths will be involved. There will be no more selfish intentions, lies, fraud, waste or abuse." Eduardo slowly walked in front of the main screen. The crew continued with their duties not paying much attention to the two, except for two security guards who looked in all directions.

"Well since you put it that way. What will you do after all this, retire?" Stargazer managed a smile.

"I plan to take a trip to Mars and see what all the hoopla is about." Eduardo returned the smirk.

"Why are you trusting me so much? Did your telepaths tell you I could be trusted?"

"Like I said, you were being disruptive down there. Considering your unique powers, I thought it best to have you up here and help out." His charismatic implications were hard to resist.

"And if I say no?"

"I won't hold it against you, but I thought you might like meeting someone before you decide." Eduardo turned to face the main screen.

A dark phantom like bubble entered the bridge six feet in size. "Quatris?" Stargazer recognized the costume and face from all the research he conducted about all the superhumans that hit the news.

Quatris' hair was pure white, half way down to his shoulder, but it had a brilliance denoting power instead of old age. His muscular stature was menacing to world class body builders, similar to Rat Bastard. The difference in appearance was due to the skintight tunic which seemed to have been woven from some super alloy Stargazer had not seen before. His white glow in his pupils reminded him of Cyer and a chill down his back. "Considering I never heard of you until two days ago. Hi, I'm Quatris." He extended a hand.

Stargazer stood up, stepped forward and shook his hand. "Hi, I'm Stargazer... wait, what... two days ago? How long has it been since the helicopter?"

"I would say about three days." Eduardo casually stated.

"I was out for three days?" Stargazer had trouble believing it.

"Well, I told my telepaths to keep you under; until Quatris showed up and convinced me you would behave." Eduardo sat in his chair looking at the main screen.

"Rebecca told me what you and your friends did. I understand your concerns, but I have to say that the Earth is in more danger than people know. The Pylaxian Empire created planet destroyers a while ago. The empire has been defeated, but Earth will be attacked soon as a means to get back at the human race... In particular it's hateful backlash at me and the other humans who protected the galaxy." Quatris' tone was very humble, unlike his usual commanding presence.

"So Eduardo knew about this danger and planned to fix it by taking over the planet?"

Quatris smiled. "No, Eduardo knew about the alien influence after I knew they planned world domination."

"But so far, we have only taken three quarters of the planet." Eduardo turned his head toward Stargazer. "The United States surrendered eight hours ago. Besides, do you really think we would get away with a forced takeover without Quatris or Hellfire's approval, not to mention Joshua and several others?" Eduardo said as most all the bridge crew paused their work for a brief moment; listening to the history lesson.

Stargazer looked at the screens on consoles and down toward Europe. "So Australia is using alien technology?"

"To a certain degree; the Pylaxians would not have given them technology out in the open. Otherwise, Argonian scouts would have reported it and they would have come to weed out any technological advantage." Quatris said, but failed to mention he and the Guardians would also be directly involved.

"Why don't you destroy the capital with your laser weapons?"

"Like I said, we aren't blood thirsty. They have millions of people in the city who are following a leadership they believe is right. Our particle accelerators are used to destroy weapons of mass destruction and weapons that will force us to use lethal means." Eduardo explained.

"So the ballistic missiles, air defense systems and aircraft on the ground were the prime targets." Stargazer softly muttered.

"Now that you're understanding what's going on, will you help us?" Eduardo swiveled his chair, facing him.

"I will sit here and relax for a while. But it would help if you can show me how you communicate and identify things on the ground." Stargazer pointed at one of the targeting consoles used to manage weapon delivery systems.

Eduardo smiled and motioned Stargazer to move to a console at his rear left. "Of course, you can stand next to Commander Isol; he will explain what he does."

Stargazer moved up to the commander. "You're American?"

"Yes, I'm from Huston, Texas, but I like Argentina better." He half smiled as he moved into position to show Stargazer his console.

The commander was in his seventies, but he was definitely in shape as a veteran of an unfortunate war.

Quatris walked up next to Eduardo. "So, when is Estabon going to come up and join us?"

"He's on the Andromeda as we speak."

"Really, that was quick for a normal human." Quatris was impressed knowing South American technology was better in some areas when compared to the Argonian Empire, but not in atmospheric to space technology.

"Well, we do our best." Eduardo said with a straight mouth then smiled.

Chapter Eighteen

••◆••

Five Days After Monday

Fiji Islands

Nature ignored world events and focused on the cycle of life as a downpour complicated low lying areas. It was dark and late into the night as the sky lit up into a bright green kem light appearance. The coolness of the night air turned warm as Mathew and the rest of the team rushed out of the building to look up at the green sky. "They're here." Lee said as Cindy transmitted their arrival through the comlink.

"Where?" Diana asked as everyone looked in all directions. The dark clouds were easy to see now, but their potency was greatly diminished as the green glow took center stage.

"There." Lee pointed to the south.

Mathew stood at the ready facing the direction but at ground level. "Show yourselves!"

Six superhumans and one android appeared twenty meters from them. "Don't attack the assassin. He's on our side." Lee warned knowing Io would be attacked if he didn't say anything, thinking Cindy or Creator would have given the warning.

"Greetings." Richard said.

Lightning and thunder roared across the sky giving Creator an impressive entry, for a least the first few seconds.

"Did you do that?" Kyle asked.

Rat Bastard and Ghost looked up, the visual bringing despair. "So that's how the sky was green." Rat Bastard said with concern.

"No, the Australians are doing that." Ghost said.

"And we have to stop them. It's time we work together to keep the aliens from winning." Richard walked up to Mathew and Valerie. Cindy walked by his side.

"You know us?" Mathew asked as stood within arm's reach of the famous crime fighter.

'It doesn't matter now, but it's good to finally meet you." Richard said remembering the two while investigating one of the bank jobs the guild had performed before Mathew took over Lanhurst's empire.

"Team this is Mirage, my sister." Lee said as his energy suit was black except for his helmet, which was not yet fully activated.

"Hi everyone, this is Creator, Night and these are Ghost, Spot, Io and Rat Bastard." Cindy hugged Lee, his suit opening up to allow her to touch him.

The rain stopped being replaced with intense humidity in the few minutes since the green field went up.

"Well it's nice to finally meet you." Diana stepped in between them.

"This is Diana." Lee turned and wrapped an arm around Diana.

"Lee, told me a lot about you." Cindy's smile was inspiring.

"Really?" Diana's interest was kindled.

"Sorry to be a party crasher, but we have much to do and I have a feeling this green sky is just the start of it." Richard stood in the middle of the ten superhumans.

"The atmospheric temperature is dramatically increasing." Lee read his optics data on his visor being in full energy suit mode.

"They're going to burn the Earth into oblivion." Rat Bastard's smashed his teeth.

"Io, is that true?" Richard turned to Io.

"I was not purveyed to the method of this force field generator; however, it is highly likely they will kill all living creatures on the planet and use Tantalized units to prevent an effective countermeasure against their efforts."

"We plan on going to Apex and ending all this. Do you guys have anything that will help us?" Mathew asked looking at Richard.

"Io." Richard uttered.

"Apex proper is forty-nine miles in diameter, populated by .356 million superhumans with abilities ranging from minor regeneration, enhanced senses to flight. The South American military force will be able to handle the superhumans; however, the three thousand plus Tantalized androids." Io turned a slight smirk and glance at Cindy. "They will be used to protect the city and device which is probably co-located in the city. The androids will be able to defeat the South American forces. However, according to the readings, the green energy field will hamper their ability to organize a viable assault on Apex before all wildlife is terminated." Io stated.

"I assume he has an extensive map of Apex?" Mathew asked.

"We all do." Richard raised his comlink to his chest.

"We lost satellite communications; probably due to all this." Lee pointed up at the bright green sky.

"Okay, let's get going then. We can iron out communicating on the way there." Mathew said.

"Do you have anything yet?" Spot whispered into Ghost's ears.

"You know half of the people here can hear us, so no need to whisper; but no, nothing yet." Ghost whispered back.

"We should have asked the South Americans." Rat Bastard grabbed Ghost's hand.

"Where ever he is, it's not near us." Ghost said and turned his group invisible, except for Io.

"So how do we do follow each other?" Ghost said.

"We don't. Everyone gather Valerie will shrink us. Lee and Kyle will fly us there undetected."

"Really?" Ghost turned his group visible again.

The men and women held hands with eight shrinking into the size of match box. "So, you guys stole the stealth fighter?" Richard turned to Mathew.

"It's a long story but yes." Mathew breathed a sigh of regret.

"After all of this is over, you and I are going to have many stories to say." Richard's shades disappeared showing off his black eyeballs.

"How long can Valerie keep us this small?" Night asked as they flew into Lee's front chest pocket.

"A few hours with this many people." Mathew replied.

"You can let go of each other's hands now, but don't separate from Lee's clothing. When it's time to leave, we need to hold hands again." Valerie instructed.

"How are we going to lose contact with the clothing?" Spot asked as all of them were shoulder to shoulder crammed at the bottom of Lee's pocket.

The darkness of the space was replaced with everything going turning a fluid transparent glass.

"Wow, is this how a bee feels?" Night said.

Lee bolted into the sky hitting Mach 6 in record time. They neared the green energy field, but didn't enter it. "Guys, this energy field is going to mess with my optics if I get inside of it. I will slow down and fly lower. We will need to also fly very low once we get above Australia." Lee reported on the comlink frequency.

"How much time do we have?" Mathew asked.

"Half a day; maybe less at this rate." Lee replied viewing the progress of the green field's affect on the atmosphere.

"You think we can stop these guys?" Kyle asked Lee as he held on to Lee's hand.

"I don't know, but I'm sure we're going to give them hell." Lee smiled with confidence.

Aboard the UFSD Tarsus, Stargazer spent a while in the bridge with Commander Isol as the men scanned the water surface around Australia. The Commander's point of view was somewhat simple letting the computer do almost all of the work as they looked for submarines. He could zoom in on the water or ground, but it was like looking at a map not knowing what you were looking at or know where you were at any point. The computer knew characteristics associated with weapon systems, people, terrain, animals, structures, anomalies, camouflaging screens and locations. An alert would pop up and Isol would zoom into the possible target to confirm its identify and activity. He would also provide an active fire command or divert it to higher approval. Stargazer however, saw it a different way as he was used to zooming in on distant objects to include seeing through materials. What he didn't have was a computer to help him look at important locations or objects. The weapons console was very impressive, but he had many more questions. Eduardo took the initiative to assign a liaison officer to escort Stargazer around the ship. Quatris stayed in the bridge attending to surveying the war as if it was his responsibility to referee the event.

"I'm sorry for you having to baby-sit me." Stargazer told his liaison, Commander Sanchez.

"Councilmember Eduardo told me to escort you. It is part of my duties as a security officer, so don't feel bad about it." Her English was impeccable and her blonde hair and blue eyes would have fooled anyone to believe she was European or North American.

"How did you get chosen to be a security officer?" Stargazer asked while they were in the elevator."

"I volunteered and completed for the position. As a matter of fact, everyone on the ship volunteered." She pressed the 14th level button, instead using the voice command.

"I'm very impressed by the achievements and accomplishments you guys have done, but do you think it will work after the war is over?"

"I was a baby when Colombia united South America. I didn't have a choice in my government, but I'm glad the federation was organized the way it was. I know many people think they should be able to do whatever they please or go the opposite way with rules that tell you how to tie your shoes. I know what the telepaths did for me and to me, and I do have a choice on whether to follow a destructive path, or do my part in a better life for future generations." The elevator stopped at the desired level, both of them walking down a corridor filled with large rooms on both sides, a large window on the doors showing the inside.

Sanchez explained what the people in the rooms did, short of logistical nightmares on the ship; they also managed all interaction for actions of one legion on the ground.

Stargazer looked at the thousands of laser communications and optical arrays connected to each room full of two dozen operators. The day was spent in awe as he witnessed the complexity of a ship on a fixed orbit over the Pacific Ocean. Stargazer was in other spaceships in the past, but this was different. The technology might not have been as smooth with a perfect gravity inside a ship that could warp beyond the speed of light; but this was in many ways pioneering technology, which made the ship and people special. Now he could understand how the first people into space were so honored and happy to be inside such a crude space capsule and have such a small view portal to see through.

After many hours it occurred to him as Sanchez asked about his friends. "Commander, I have been missing for three days. Is there a way I can contact my friends?"

"It 's possible if you have a telephone number or address?"

"Oh..." Stargazer looked down at the comlink he wished he hadn't traded away, even though it would've been destroyed when he made contact with the gunship's unusually harden armor. "All I know is the Octavian Farm in Fort Lauderdale or if all fails, can you contact SIA headquarters?" Stargazer stared at Sanchez's light blue eyes.

"I will see what I can do." She smiled, but she seemed concerned about having to get authorization to be able to allow a communiqué with SIA.

"I also need to talk to Quatris. I forgot to tell him something about a super being gunning for him."

"Should we be worried about that?" Sanchez raised an eyebrow.

"It's a future event, so probably not." Stargazer replied.

"You can tell the future?" Sanchez doubted.

"No, I just know a little bit of his future, because I went thousands of years into the future." He stated.

"Interesting and how was Earth?" She placed her hands on her waistline.

"I don't know; I was in the Andromeda galaxy at the time."

"Boy, are you sure you were there, because that requires a lot of faith to believe?"

"Yeah, it does, but you had to be there yourself to understand. By the way, you wouldn't happen to know anyone named Alexmarks, would you?"

"I'm sure that are thousands of Alex Marks in the world."

Stargazer looked at her, it never dawned on him that Alex Marks was two names meaning King Alex Marks was somewhere on the planet. He would have continued with his logic, on why Alex Marks was allowing all of the events to occur, but Cassandra's explanation about free will was enough for him to give up. "Yeah, I suppose there are. Anyways, since you are my guide, what should I know if something happens to the ship, safety wise?"

"Each level and every area is compartmented every thirty feet. If there is a gradual or sudden lost of atmosphere the compartment would automatically be isolated. Any person underneath a vacuum door will be allotted time to move out of the way. Each crewmember carries a helmet to be able to survive without an atmosphere for about an hour, before having to connect to an oxygen supply, if the atmosphere is not restored within the hour." Sanchez showed him her helmet and a nearby box inside the wall containing tubes to connect to the helmet.

"I see, what about a fire?" Stargazer continued to ask scenarios while she provided satisfying answers.

Time passed as they moved to many sections of the ship; until the lighting of the room they entered turned a slow flashing red along with a buzzing sound. "Red Alert, all hands to battle stations!" The alarm repeated three times, the lights returned to normal but the buzzing continued for a minute.

"Take me to the bridge." Stargazer commanded, knowing Sanchez would not be able to tell him why the alarm was sounded.

She ran down the corridors, several people crisscrossing their path without issues as if they planned to pass by. Once they entered the elevator Sanchez spoke. "Commander Sanchez and Mr. Stargazer, Bridge."

The elevator swiftly moved three times faster than its normal operation. The boots gripped tight inside the elevator keeping them from lifting off the ground as it moved and stopped at its destination. Stargazer knew it was a matter of voltage to the magnets inside the floor. The doors slide open and they entered the bridge. Stargazer saw the main screen then peered through the ship confirming he shouldn't have doubted that a green energy field covered Earth.

Quatris stood next to Eduardo's chair. He turned to see the two additions to the bridge. "It has begun... I recommend you move your ships as far as possible from the field. It acts like an EMP if anything electrical comes in contact with it."

"Sir, we can't see or communicate through the field." The navigator reported.

"Yeah, that too." Quatris casually added.

A corner of Eduardo's mouth curled up. "Commander Hobbs, tell the fleet to pull back past three thousand miles. Get me the Battlestar captains so we can see if our fighters can penetrate the field and send messages to our ground forces." Eduardo turned his head towards Quatris. "I assume you and other superhumans can go back and forth between the field without too much trouble?"

"Yes, but."

"Yes, I know, you can't go down there for long, in case a Seer Spirit shows up and we can't tell you." Eduardo turned back to see the main screen. "Stargazer, can you see through the energy field?"

Stargazer focused his vision, peering through the energy field with relative ease. "Yes, I can, why?"

"Because I need an answer right now if you can help us. If not, then Commander Sanchez can take you to your room, unless you want to go down there and look for your friends?" Eduardo coldly said.

Quatris glared at Stargazer as if also waiting for an answer.

"You probably knew I could see through that field didn't you." Stargazer fixed his gaze at Eduardo's head.

Eduardo turned to face him. "I didn't know, but hoped it would be true... Will you help us?"

Stargazer inhaled some air. "What do you want me to do?"

"Rick, let Stargazer take your spot. Get another chair and help him find what we're looking for. If things work the way they do, we should be able to still fire our weapons through the field. But don't worry Steve; we only use our particle accelerators against non-living targets."

Commander Isol looked at Stargazer as he approached the seat. "So you're Steve?"

"And you're Rick?"

"Let's get to work." Rick Isol's happiness came from Stargazer's willingness to help them in a time of need.

"Quatris grinned a little and looked out into space in thought.

"Helmsman, take us out four thousand miles and maintain orbit over Australia." Eduardo commanded as the fleet adapted to the situation, with the battle destroyer moving swiftly into position.

Chapter Nineteen

••◆••

The Stadium

P olice officers and national guard soldiers maintained orderly lines with many people seeming to come from the streets more for shelter than the vigil itself. The vigil in the name of prayer and hope for peace reflected a populace in denial and fear; having been unable to defend their homes from a superpower able to neutralize their military and defiant citizens. The open carry policy would have helped in combating terrorism, rioting or even regular military forces, but the lack of South American boots on the ground in major cities left many citizens either fighting themselves over food and shelter or uniting together with ignorance about their supposed enemy.

A short trimmed bearded man stood in line with his hands crossed. His shabby caterpillar heavy blue parka had not seen a washing machine for a week with several coffee and dirt stains marking his elbows and mid waist. His body was clean apart from his clothing. The brown uncombed hair and strong eyes gave him a rugged look, but his slight smile and posture suggested a dignity only a person who had been through very hard times and survived could carry.

He stared forward, but picked up his head and eyes towards the ceiling windows above. He wasn't looking specifically at the ceiling, as he turned to the rear, getting out of line as if he heard or smelled something in the crowd of people waiting or moving about the concourse entrance.

He worked his way through the crowd, seeing a young girl sitting by an ATM. The teen wore a flimsy coat, but stylish for the occasion. Her attention was on people taking money out of the working ATM. With a blue enzyme twill cap worn at a slant, she surveyed the people as if analyzing their potential or weaknesses.

The man walked up to the ATM line, several people in front of him suddenly stepped out of line as if they had something better else to do. The teen's hazel teal eyes noticed the people's reactions, but she didn't look into the man's face. Instead, she stared at the shoes of the people in line as if she was figuring out shoe sizes. It wasn't long before the man stood in front of the ATM. The girl took a casual glimpse of his face, but didn't expect his eyes to meet hers.

She quickly turned away playing with her long sandy brown hair as if the side of her head itched.

The man moved up as the girl focused her attention away from the ATM. The machine beeped and hissed with paper. The man moved to the side; his hiker's boots touching her sneakers.

She almost jumped back and looked up to see the man's hand full of twenty dollar bills extended out to her.

"You can have this money, it's on me."

"Who said I need money?" Her choked reply seemed awkward.

"Take it Jenny." His voice was strong and soft at the same time.

"How do you know my name?" Her eyes widen with fear.

"I know everything." The man pushed six hundred dollars into her coat pocket, turned around and walked away.

Jenny quickly stuffed her hand into the pocket making sure none of the money escaped as she raced after the dark blue parka.

"Mister!" She fought herself through the crowd of a dozen people grabbing his wrist. "Wait. Where are you going?"

The man turned to face her. Then turned his head toward the center of the stadium. "I'm going that way."

"Who are you?" She held tighter onto his parka sleeve.

"I'm Joshua." His smile revealed white well kept teeth.

"Can I go with you?" Jenny let go of him, now that she had his full attention.

"You shouldn't talk to strangers."

"I don't have anywhere else to go." Jenny looked off to the sides expecting someone else to look at her or them, but the people within arm's reach away seemed to be deaf or completely apathetic.

Joshua offered her his hand. "Yes, I know... Okay, let's get in line, something special is about to happen and we're going to have a front row seat."

Jenny's soul was open to him as if he really did know she was an orphan and a recent runaway. With a trusting heart she followed Joshua through the crowd and patiently waited by his side in line.

Neuron scanners cleared people entering the six appointed main entrances into the Dallas Cowboy's home stadium. Wide plasma screens seen from most locations in all level concourses made for an exciting media hub many people wished to experience during the season, but this was an off year; thanks to the invasion. In retrospect, it was business for executives and a declaration of resistance for others. People poured into the complex as word got out about the United States' surrender to South America. The stadium event was one of hope for peace, with many speakers and services provided on the field.

There was no face to face interaction between President Dover and Council-members, or ink signing of documents. But the digital acknowledgement by Congress, Senate and President Dover over a video conference and transmitted signatures made the process as ironclad as many legal contracts. Some states defied the surrendering authorities, with Texas being one state on the verge of civil anarchy. Many rallies and events in the cities were an attempt to bring people together instead of siding with pockets of rebellion in the face of uncertainty.

"I'm a little hungry." Jenny mentioned just before walking through the sensors.

"We'll grab some food and water upstairs."

The two made their way to a vendor. Joshua casually looked around as if he was interested in the surroundings for their beauty or splendor, a notable contrast to everyone else with grim eyes or cheeky fake smiles. Even Jenny was full of bleak thoughts before he came on the screen.

The more she stood by his side and watched his peaceful resolve, the safer she felt. Two scoops of chocolate ice cream on a waffle cone started their trek to the stadium stands. "I already ate two chili dogs." Jenny objected.

"It's going to get hot outside, plus I know it's your favorite." Joshua replied licking his strawberry covered cone.

The awes and silence from half of the sixty thousand people in the stadium turned everyone's heads up at the ceiling and sky. The sky gradually changed color from sky blue to light blue, then bright green. Everything around seemed to change hues as the green mixed in with the environment. An up roar of yelling and loud talking was followed by loud speaker announcements. "Ladies and gentlemen, please be calm. The stadium roof is being closed for your safety. We are looking into what is causing the green aura in the sky. For, now please do not panic. If you wish to leave the stadium, please do so in an orderly fashion. Once again please do not panic."

"We need to hurry." Joshua lightly grabbed Jenny's arm.

"Why, they said not to panic." She licked her ice cream a little quicker trying to keep it from melting.

"But they will once they figure out no one has cell-phone service." Joshua walked while people moved out of the way as if they were told beforehand that someone was trying to get through.

They sat along the middle row on the south side, as people panicked complaining about their lack of internet access and communication with family and friends.

Doleful and fearful faces looked all around while Jenny focused her stare up at the green sky. "What could it be?"

"A pressure cooker for a lack of better words." Joshua replied taking out a bottle of water from his inside pocket.

He took off his parka and folded it into a cushion and sat on it. "You might want to get comfortable. It's going to be a long day."

"What's going on?" Jenny also removed her coat, the temperature in the dome slowly countering the increase in heat.

"The Australians are trying to cleanse the world."

"Isn't South America bad enough?"

"Oh, wait until I tell you about the superhumans and the aliens." Joshua said finishing his cone.

"What? Who are you?" Jenny's despondent confusion showed in her temporarily contorted face.

"Let me tell you a story about a young woman named Evelyn. She was about your age when she met a naive and young factory worker. Her eyes were beautiful, full of love and joy. A queen would have given up her kingdom for a fraction of Evelyn's magnificent golden hair..."

Jenny listened intently, ignoring the speakers on the stage down on the far end of the field and people moving about trying to get comfortable after announcements stated it wasn't safe outside in the open due to the green field.

Joshua ended the tail an hour later, Jenny's partially dried tears wetting her raised long sleeves. "So you can save everyone? Right?"

Joshua glared into her eyes. "I have, but not as everyone would like it to happen, in a brimstone and fire kind of way. Everyone will be involved and will remember what will occur today and see a new future unfold."

"Why did you pick me to be here with you?" Jenny wisely surmised.

"People will forget over time, but you and some others will remember and keep the peace... For now, what this world needs is a final battle in a war destined to change all living beings on Earth and many other planets in the universe." Joshua lightly placed his hand on hers, as the green glow above grew stronger.

"How will South America beat the aliens?"

"They're not alone, the Eternal Champions, the Five Ghosts, EFL, the Guild with no Name; even a rare alliance with the ultimate assassins will turn the tide. The hope of Earth lies with them, and us." Joshua smiled, closed his eyes and crossed his leg as if imagining a football game in action.

Jenny felt intense fatigue as she looked out across the seating and field. Everyone in the stadium slowly collapsed where they sat or stood, except for pregnant women, mothers with babies, the handicapped and toddlers and their parents. Joshua glowed with a white aura as if about to ascend into heaven.

The quietness of the stadium was calming; even the infants succumbed to the sudden change in relaxing ambiance. The calmness was transparent to the heroes moving in on Apex as all people small and large, young and old; saw Joshua's face in their thoughts. "People of Earth, I am Joshua, most of you have taken your lives for granted. A society based on rules which you used for your own gain or pleasure. There are those who decided to make a difference, to fight evil to the last breath. Australia unwittingly sided with an evil plot to exterminate all living beings on the planet. South America's vision to fight for the little guy is only an extension of many humans and superhumans… superheroes, who have been fighting for you to live and exist. Now you will witness what these heroes have gone through so you could have peace and joy in a world without prejudice, hatred, greed, selfish envy and lack." Joshua showed seven billion people the victories and defeats of all the superheroes' past to the present.

Jenny sat up, quickly regaining her strength. The visions and experiences of all the heroes since Neutronium to the most recent, Io; occurred in a matter of minutes. She looked around seeing everyone else was in a state of animation, even the infants, and the green sky was not getting any brighter. She faced Joshua who calmly sat looking at her waking up.

"I told you we had front row seats. Sit back and watch." Joshua looked out onto the field and smiled, but what he and Jenny saw wasn't the field full of people, but a third person point of view of a boy in the middle of his 5th grade class; daydreaming.

Author Notes

◆◆◆◆◆

Over the last few years I re-published "Creator" and "He Is Known as Ego". In addition, I set off to write and publish the remaining six books of the series. It's with great pleasure that I was able to write the books to this point. I self-published with various companies and know there are minor editing issues in all of the books with grammar, spelling and a few formatting errors; but I also know that my readers have loved all of the books with an eagerness of seeing an epic story come alive.

Normal superhero books are in the form of a comic or some form of video/movie type of media. This book I hope like the others has opened a world of possibilities for storytelling and entertainment. I want to point this out, because this particular book is part one of the last two books in the series as an epic story all by themselves. I thought about putting the entire story in one book, but wanted to give the reader the opportunity to see things from different perspectives. Book seven covers the perspective of Stargazer's and Mathew's group, while the last book "Last Hope for Earth," goes into two perspectives which is from the Ramirez brothers and the overall good guys at the end. I did this because the superheroes are scattered prior to the final battle and in the battle which takes place on Earth and in space. There are a lot of characters involved from all the books into these last two books. I hope the list of characters has helped in keeping you from being completely confused and frustrated as to who is who.

I must apologize for the abrupt ending to this book. I myself hate movies that end in the middle of a battle, but there was no getting around this transition from book seven to book eight. Once again I didn't want to make one long book and change perspectives and timeframes, which if you read book eight, it starts with the Ramerize brothers during the mid 1960s. I debated on having Joshua's actions in book eight, but decided to place it in seven for the purpose of telling the story with a cleaner jump from hero to hero in the battle for Apex.

I tend to get some criticism about the descriptions of the characters, like height, eye color and hair color. Usually an author will pick out unique descriptive attributes that stand out from all the rest. Well, I in a way wanted for the superheroes to stand out in the aspects of their normal appearance, since they are much like "Superman" with perfect rows of teeth and super hair strands sort of speaking. I tried to focus on the costumes, voices and eye colors because that is one thing people want to know and remember; apart from the powers and abilities the superhumans and normal humans possess. So when you read about how not over weight or not short a person is, it's because they are superhumans who can eat and almost never gain weight. Or they are like Creator, a shape shifter who can look like any which way he wants to. But I did make an effort to point out the Elven ears and black eyeballs. Unlike, Stargazer and his group who are all tall normal men, except for Rat Bastard who would pass for a tall world champion body builder. So, I hope it was easy for you to distinguish between the characters and follow the storyline without too much difficulty.

My last note is on the art book cover. I played around with different artist in the past for covers and learned how to use many Adobe programs in my studies for web and graphic design. With the help of Photoshop, I was able to create the cover I wanted; to include the font structure and bullet moving through the center of the text at an angle in the main title. My attempt was to make it different then other book cover artwork, at the same time taking into account the primary basics of attracting an audience. In this case, the first impression of an eye catching image and title. In addition, I wanted it to mirror the last book which has the good guy as the focus, while this art book cover is focused on the bad guy which is one of many ultimate assassins.

I want to encourage those aspiring writers of any genre to never stop writing. It is easy to write a sentence or an essay for a required class or work project. Writing is a skill which is developed through some study, but it is also an art which is developed by writing and more writing. I have written a book about creating and publishing printed and digital works. If you do come across my book, I am sure it will help you in how you write. Most importantly, it will I hope give you a better grasp that writing as an art is all about telling the story; by showing the story. I hope you have seen how I show the story in many different ways. The superhero books are intended to show you behind the scenes information which our main characters are totally unaware of. Some people don't like the third person point-of-view all knowing, but all knowing narration does not mean the reader knows everything. There has to be some degree of mystery for everything, otherwise story telling would be boring and I hope I conveyed enough mystery while giving a storyline that is not centered on the hero or one hero alone.

I want to thank you again for taking the time to dwell in the world of superhumans. I hope you enjoyed reading this book and will continue to read the last book in the series, "Last Hope for Earth".

www.ingramcontent.com/pod-product-compliance
Lightning Source LLC
Chambersburg PA
CBHW070816120626
46556CB00002B/526